CHAIN OF COMMAND

CHAIN
OF
COMMAND

A CORPS JUSTICE NOVEL
BOOK 9 OF THE CORPS JUSTICE SERIES

C. G. COOPER

To my loyal group of Novels Live warriors and Beta Readers,
thanks for your help in crafting this novel.
To our amazing troops serving all over the world,
thank you for your bravery and service.
And especially to the United States Marine Corps.
Keep taking the fight to the enemy.
Semper Fidelis
- CGC -

CHAPTER 1

A refreshing breeze blew in across the small lake that separated the Disney Yacht Club Resort from Epcot and the Boardwalk retail strip. The cool seventy-degree morning did little to dissuade the grandkids from building mountains and forts in the hotel's sand-filled swimming pool. The three-acre water paradise was like a magnet. It drew in every kid who clamored by their parents' bedside whenever the sun came up.

He watched his four grandsons and one granddaughter as they switched from building to destruction. The youngest, Lily, boisterous with her blonde curls and swim-diaper-stuffed swimsuit, squealed as her brothers and cousins smashed and swept their creations away.

He smiled as they played, savoring each moment. He laughed with them. There had been too many lost moments over the years. Some were inevitable, some self-imposed. Best not to lose more.

1

His hand reached over and touched his wife's leg. She was engrossed in the latest Danielle Steel novel, seemingly not noticing the goings-on in the pool. But he knew better. She was a good mom, a terrific grandmother. She could hear a cry from across the house or detect danger as it was happening, a modern day supermom. Like so many military wives, she'd learned to adapt, to play the role of mother and father while her husband was away.

Without looking away from her book, she set her hand on top of his. It wasn't as smooth as it used to be, or as soft as the first time he'd felt it, but he loved it just the same. If the past month had taught him anything, it was that family was important, possibly the most important. He sighed.

It hadn't been easy. His two sons had grown up on bases all over the world, following him as he climbed the ranks. He understood their bitterness. They'd never had a home, always traveling, always moving.

But things were better now. He'd made an effort to reconnect, whereas in the past he probably would have buried himself in work. He wouldn't take the credit, though. It was his wife who'd finally given him the ultimatum.

She'd dealt with the missteps, the poor communication and the open-ended deployments, but she drew the line at her family.

"You're about to lose them," she'd said with that hard Southern edge he'd come to associate with her mother. "You either fix this or I leave."

They'd railed back and forth. He told her he was doing it all for her even though he knew just as the words left his mouth that it wasn't true. He loved the uniform, the challenge.

He thought that maybe after a day or two she would back down, see the error of her demands.

But she hadn't and he was glad for it.

They'd been in Florida for almost a week. Breakfasts in bed or lobster omelets at the Captain's Grille. During the day they'd traversed the Magic Kingdom and worn out the rides as the grandkids begged for the next amusement. Lily loved the Peter Pan ride and Grant preferred Thunder Mountain. At night they ate at the Beaches and Cream Soda Shop, sharing the enormous Kitchen Sink sundae for dessert. Lily giggled as he stuffed spoon after spoon into his mouth. They hadn't come close to finishing the whopping sugar creation, but he'd tried for them.

While the kids napped, he corralled his sons and spent the time getting to know them again. His oldest was a school teacher, soon-to-be a principal. The second was back in school getting his law degree after a disappointing run as a financial planner. Neither had followed him into the service, and now he knew why.

For years he'd been bitter about that fact. They were both fit, gifted athletes and natural leaders. They would've done well in the service, fighting for their country. Instead they'd taken after their mother, gone the liberal route, often taunting him with their politics.

He didn't care anymore. His wife was right. All that mattered was that they were together at last. One family.

The kids were changed and the adults were trying to herd them into the jogging strollers. Lily was the only one cooperating, a fact that made him smile. He bent down and hugged her, receiving a wet kiss on the nose in response.

"I love you, Grapa," she said, still not able to pronounce "Grandpa" properly.

"I love you too, sweetie."

He kissed her on the forehead.

"So we'll meet you at the French cafe in an hour," his wife said, stuffing snacks in her purse.

"I'll see you there," he replied.

"Are you sure you won't come with us now?" she asked, her tone clearly indicating what she thought about his other commitment.

"It won't be long, honey, I promise."

It was a lie, but she didn't seem to notice.

"Okay. Don't forget to put on some sunscreen," she said.

He nodded and then kissed her on the lips, moving in for a hug. He savored the smell of mint shampoo and the perfume he'd bought for her the day before. In that moment he realized how much he loved her, how much he needed her. He couldn't let go.

"Um, honey, the kids are leaving," she said.

"Right."

He let her go and stepped back, smiling.

"Love you, honey."

She smiled back and took off after the family.

He watched them go.

When they'd finally made it over the bridge leading into the international entrance of Epcot, he turned and headed back to the room.

He emerged five minutes later and left out the front entrance, nodding to the hotel's greeter in his ship captain's uniform.

The prayer came to him as he walked, a snippet remembered from some long ago sermon.

Lord, forgive my thoughts, my actions and my words.

Before he knew it, he was surrounded by prickly palmettos and towering pines. The busy roadways were far behind. He had no idea how long it had taken him to walk to where he now stopped, but there he was, at the spot.

There'd been a lot of hikes over the years. Back-breaking rucksacks and sweat-filled boots. Perspiration and blood. He and his men, one foot in front of the other.

He thought of it now with nostalgic reverence as he fell to his knees, the emotion threatening to overwhelm his resolve. Images of his wife, his sons, his grandkids around the periphery as he sank further into the gloom. Then came his men who had died, given their lives for their country or for the brother standing next to him. *Please, God, watch over them.*

He took a deep breath and reached into his pocket. It was time.

The Assistant Commandant of the Marine Corps put the barrel of the Colt 1911 in his mouth and pulled the trigger.

CHAPTER 2

Cal Stokes waited as his host finished the phone call. The former Marine staff sergeant didn't wait on many people. He was the silent owner of Stokes Security International (SSI), a company founded by his now-deceased father. SSI assigned expert former military operators to corporations and governments all over the world, and they raked in millions every year. He was now the de facto leader of The Jefferson Group.

In the public eye, The Jefferson Group was a consultancy that provided a wide range of expertise ranging from network stability to personal security. Their real mission was only known to a handful of people.

Sanctioned by the President of the United States, Brandon Zimmer, the warriors of The Jefferson Group operated out of Charlottesville, Virginia, executing secret missions in the States and overseas. In short, they were President Zimmer's black asset. Untraceable and highly effective.

The Commandant of the Marine Corps, General Scott Winfield, hung up the phone and exhaled.

"Anything new, sir?" asked Cal. The Assistant Commandant of the Marine Corps, General Douglas Ellwood, had disappeared while on vacation two days before. Search parties were combing Lake Buena Vista, led by local NCIS agents.

Gen. Winfield nodded. "They found him."

"He's dead."

Another slow nod.

"It looks like suicide."

Cal's stomach turned. He'd recommended that Gen. Ellwood not be allowed to go to Florida, but the Commandant overruled him. One of those unwritten rules between comrades. "You were right," said Winfield.

The normally upright warrior looked deflated, his face drawn.

"You had no idea that he would do that, sir."

"I should have. You did."

Cal didn't reply. Nearly a month earlier, at the Marine Corps Birthday Ball held at Marine Barracks 8th & I, Gen. Winfield and his good friend, Gen. McMillan, USMC, who also happened to be the Chairman of the Joint Chiefs, informed Cal of a new threat to the Marine Corps. The punchline from Winfield had been simple. "We believe that come this time next year, there will no longer be a United States Marine Corps."

At first Cal blamed the booze. The two generals had been at the sauce for hours. But as they outlined the situation, and asked for his assistance, he couldn't help but believe them.

The Marine Corps had faced disbanding in the past, most recently in the early 20th century. But World War II and the raising of the flag on Mount Suribachi had changed that. In fact, it was James Forrestal, the Secretary of the Navy, who'd said in 1945, *"The raising of that flag on Suribachi means a Marine Corps for the next five hundred years."*

Apparently not.

It had been the Assistant Commandant of the Marine Corps himself who'd brought the danger to Winfield's attention. Incredibly, Gen. Ellwood confessed to being an unwitting participant in the plot to slash the Marine Corps out of existence.

Now on loan to the Commandant with the blessing of the president, Cal had pressed for an in-depth investigation. Gen. Winfield preferred a more cautious approach, saying, "If General Ellwood was part of this, he will be held accountable. I don't want to ruin his career if we don't have to."

Cal almost lost his patience at that point, replying, "With respect, sir, the general has already admitted his guilt. Whether he knew what he was doing or not doesn't change a thing. You brought me in to help, to take action. I recommend you let me and my team do what we do best."

Now their key witness was dead. Cal didn't have to tell the Commandant how much time they'd lost. Gen. Winfield knew.

"I never asked, sir, was General Ellwood a friend?"

"We knew each other, of course, but I wouldn't say we were friends. My God, how could he do that with his family being so close, at Disney World for Christ's sake!"

Cal had his opinions, but he kept them to himself. Now wasn't the time to besmirch the name of a Marine general.

After taking a few moments to gather his thoughts, Winfield said, "I know we talked about you putting on the uniform again, but I think we missed that window. Can you and your team do what's needed without joining the ranks?"

Cal hadn't thought much of the Commandant's idea of him and his other former Marines going back in the Corps for the sake of the investigation. The Corps was too small. They knew too many people. They would be recognized. If there was a silver lining to Gen. Ellwood's death it was that Cal wouldn't have to pin on fake major's bars.

"We can do it, sir."

"Good. Now, how quickly can you get to Florida?"

CHAPTER 3

The score was tied seven to seven at the half. It looked liked the Army was fighting hard to settle the score from the shellacking the Navy Mids had put on them the year before. As it stood, the Navy had twelve consecutive wins in the always popular Army-Navy Game.

Exuberant fans cheered as their teams headed to the locker rooms. Maybe it would be a close game for a change.

The two men watched the changeover on the field, each remembering their time at the Naval Academy. They'd been roommates as plebes. Now, almost thirty-five years later, they sat and watched the new generation of officers.

"You going to the funeral?" asked Rear Admiral Joseph Gower, USN, adjusting the bill of his Class of 1979 ball cap.

Major General Duane Mason, USA, snorted.

"Do I have a choice?"

Gower sipped his non-alcoholic beer, frowning.

"We owe it to Doug."

10

Another snort from Mason.

"It was your idea to use him, and now you want to go to his funeral?" Mason took a long drink from his own beer. He let out a burp. "Then again, I wouldn't mind seeing Cassy again. She's still a looker after all these years."

Gower turned to face his friend. "Don't be an idiot. We need to keep up appearances. If you don't come to Quantico with me…."

Mason put up his hands. "Okay, okay. I was just kidding around. I won't even make a pass at Cassy." He chuckled and returned his gaze to the row of female midshipmen below.

Adm. Gower stared at his friend. Even after all those years, sometimes he still couldn't decide whether Duane was pulling his leg. Hell, he hadn't believed Mason when he'd told him that rather than getting his commission in the Navy, he was going to raise his right hand as an Army officer. It happened occasionally, but it still rankled the career Navy officer that he hadn't seen it coming. Duane had never gotten his sea legs, but Gower thought for sure he'd make it work.

Instead of speeding off to the fleet together, Duane Mason entered the Army pipeline, first as an infantry officer, Ranger tabbed, and then on to special operations, even a stint with Delta Forces.

He remembered the nights they'd stayed up watching the news at the Academy, the reports of Soviet incursions and subsequent expansion. They'd gnashed their teeth at the weakling, President Carter, and then rolled their eyes at the actor turned politician who promised to take the fight to the Soviets.

It wasn't the first time they'd been wrong. In fact, Reagan was a personal hero to both men, although for different reasons. Gower appreciated Reagan's resolve backed up by his never-ending cold calculation. Mason admired the man for his moxie, for giving the Russkies the middle finger and then backing it up with force.

Reagan's actions would help define the careers of both officers. While Mason ran around in jungles and jumped from the clouds, Gower endured months-long patrols under the Arctic and every ocean on earth.

They'd kept in touch, always making it back for the Army-Navy game when deployments allowed. Mason would wear his *Go Army* shirt and Gower his *Go Navy*. The winner got to keep both. Gower was racking them up.

Between duty stations, they vacationed with their families, and when nearly concurrent divorces happened, they vacationed as roommates. Sometimes there'd been a third. Another classmate from the Academy days.

Douglas Ellwood had played tailback for the Mids. They'd met when the Navy football coach assigned his star running back to the studious Gower to help raise his flagging grades.

Gower had at first thought that Ellwood was a simple-minded meathead. All he knew was football. But as their sessions progressed, Gower was surprised to find that Doug Ellwood was no moron; he'd just never learned how to learn.

Ellwood had returned the favor by introducing the socially handicapped Gower to his near-constant entourage of college co-eds. Their friendship grew and soon Mason was added to the trio. Whenever they had a free weekend, the three bolted from campus and conquered the surrounding colleges.

For four years they studied and partied. Despite the rigors and rules of the military academy, they made the best of their time together.

For a moment Gower thought back to those times, to when they'd nearly been equals. As much as he hated to admit it, he'd always been jealous of Doug, even when he walked in that first day with that stupid grin on his face. *The trusting fool.*

Time had not lessened Gower's resentment. He remembered when the letter had come from the Marine Corps (Ellwood had listed Gower as his next of kin), informing him of 1st Lt. Douglas Ellwood's wounding in Grenada. There had been genuine concern for his friend in that moment. Months later Doug would receive the Silver Star for his exploits on the small island.

So as Gower moved from submarines to shore duty and back again, always choosing and receiving the best career-advancing posts, Doug Ellwood played Marine and kept falling into mounds of rose petals. Dumb luck it would seem.

Gower never let his covetous yearnings show, always congratulating his friend on his accomplishments, even when Ellwood had been selected to be the Assistant Commandant of the Marine Corps, one step away from the throne itself. That had been the last straw.

It hadn't taken much to enlist Mason. He hated the Marines and their incessant swagger. To him the Army was more than equipped to fill in whatever puny void the Marines left behind.

Together they made a good team. Gower had the contacts and Mason owned the muscle. Gower hadn't known how much they'd need the muscle until now.

He sipped his beer, wishing it was of the alcoholic variety. Maybe after this was all finished. Just a nip.

"Everything's set on your end?" he asked.

Mason answered without taking his eyes off the cheerleaders. "Of course."

Gower nodded and slunk back into this chair. Things were finally coming together. He could almost taste victory. It was no longer the consolation prize for not picking up a third star. This was it, his new path.

He knew his days in the Navy were numbered, and he'd come to terms with that. Now he looked to the future. It seemed much brighter than it had a year before, thanks to the recently deceased Gen. Ellwood. He almost chuckled as he remembered the look on Doug's face when he'd realized how much he'd hurt his own service. The fool was still the same blubbering jock from 1976.

As he watched the opposing team retake the field, his aspirations took their customary hold in his subconscious. After all, what better way to start your new career than to be known as the architect behind the Marine Corps' undoing?

CHAPTER 4

Cal Stokes and Daniel Briggs looked like an unlikely pair. Cal was a couple inches shorter than six feet with brown hair that he kept just longer than his regulation cut in the Marine Corps. Daniel had long blonde hair that he liked to keep in a ponytail and walked with the calm stride of a Buddhist monk.

While Cal's visage leaned toward stern, or maybe just alert, Daniel walked through the world with a Zen-like quality that bordered on aloof. It wasn't that he was strange or on the fringe of society. The former Marine sniper just knew his place in the world. After struggling with PTSD, he'd found his salve: God.

As his colleagues ribbed each other like Marines just leaving Parris Island, Daniel took the quiet approach, letting things soak in.

That, coupled with his unique skills, made Daniel Briggs a permanent fixture next to his boss, Cal Stokes. The two men made a formidable team. Whether shooting their way through a throng of terrorists or maneuvering the minefields of D.C. politics, Cal and Daniel belonged side by side.

15

You could say that Cal was the heart of The Jefferson Group, but Daniel was its soul, a warrior dedicated to leaving the world a little better each day.

The two Marines approached the police tape and flashed their ID badges to the NCIS agent who looked like he'd just turned twenty-one.

"Can I help you, gentlemen?" he asked.

"We were told to ask for Special Agent Barrett?" said Cal.

Without taking his eyes off of them, the agent shouted, "Hey, Robbie, you've got visitors."

A trim guy in a golf shirt and matching shorts turned and headed their way.

"You the guys from Quantico?"

Cal nodded. "Cal Stokes and this is Daniel Briggs."

Barrett's eyes squinted as if one of their names triggered something in his memory. "Robbie Barrett, gentlemen." He shook both men's hands. Now that Cal saw him up close, he thought the guy looked more like a professional golfer than an NCIS agent. "Why don't we take a walk and I'll fill you in."

They followed Special Agent Barrett until they were out of hearing range of the rest of the NCIS investigators.

"So the Commandant sent you." It sounded more like an accusation than a simple statement.

"He did," answered Cal.

"Why you and not his staff?"

Cal shrugged. "He wanted an outside opinion."

Barrett stared at Cal for a moment, and then said, "Just so you know, I understand the needs of the Marine Corps, but I'm not about to hinder this investigation because the Corps wants to save face."

Cal resisted the urge to clench his teeth. This was Barrett's backyard, not his.

"We're just here to see what you've found, let you know that we're available to help, and report anything we think is pertinent to General Winfield."

Barrett crossed his arms over his chest. "And what makes you qualified to question my team?"

Cal exhaled. "Look, I get it. We're outsiders. You don't trust us. That's fine. But we *are* here on behalf of the Commandant of the Marine Corps. He specifically told us to behave. Me, you might have to look out for, but Snake Eyes here," Cal pointed at Daniel, "he's as tame as a kitten."

"Wait, you're that Daniel Briggs? The one who was up for the Medal of Honor?" asked Barrett, his face shifting from annoyance to curiosity.

"I didn't get it, if that's what you're asking," Daniel said simply.

"That's not what I heard. This guy I know—"

"Leave it alone, Barrett," said Cal, one of the few people who knew why his friend had turned down the Medal.

Barrett looked like he was going to press, but he didn't. Cal could tell that as soon as they left, the NCIS agent was going to make some discreet inquiries. Not that it mattered, but Cal couldn't afford to be highlighted.

"In case you were wondering, our presence here is to remain confidential, by order of the Commandant."

"I don't fall under your chain of command, Mr. Stokes."

Cal grinned. "Okay. Would a call from the president help keep your mouth shut?"

Barrett's mouth pursed, then opened, then closed again.

"Good," continued Cal. "Now, like I said, we'll stay out of your hair. The faster you tell us what's going on, the faster we go home."

"How do I know you won't—"

"I'm a Marine, Mr. Barrett."

Barrett glared at him but held his tongue. Finally, he said, "Come over to my car and I'll tell you what I know."

His car turned out to be a brand new Cadillac Escalade. The paint job was a dull matte black, a theme that continued to the vehicle's rims. Cal wondered what a thirty-something NCIS agent was doing driving such a souped-up SUV.

"Nice ride," said Daniel, who must have been thinking the same thing as Cal.

"We just confiscated it from a squid who was running an ecstasy ring out of his barracks," said Barrett, unfazed by Daniel's comment. He opened up the trunk with a click of his key fob.

There was an assortment of files neatly arranged in black plastic crates sitting next to a golf bag and a pair of recently used golf shoes. Barrett grabbed a green file and sat back against the rear bumper.

"Here's what we know so far. No signs of struggle. No recent footprints in the same vicinity. The only prints on the gun were his. The pistol itself was registered to General Ellwood in 1982. We had a brief discussion with Mrs. Ellwood, but she was justifiably upset."

"What about his sons? We heard they were down here on vacation," said Cal.

"They were clueless. Said the week was going fine. It came as a shock to all of them."

"Do you believe them?" asked Daniel.

Barrett shrugged. "I've been doing this for a while. I can usually tell if someone's holding back. They were genuinely in pain. No, I think he hid it well."

"Helluva place to do it though," observed Cal.

"Tell me about it," said Barrett. "Can't say this'll be the happiest place on Earth for those kids."

Cal nodded, trying to piece together Gen. Ellwood's motives. He and Daniel had talked about it on the way down. They even had The Jefferson Group's in-house shrink, Dr. Higgins, looking into the general's history. If anyone could dig up something on a person's psychological makeup, it was Higgins and his extensive experience as one of the CIA's top interrogators.

Before leaving for Florida, Gen. Ellwood told the Commandant that he wanted a week with his family before the storm hit. He knew that word of his involvement in the plot against the Marine Corps, no matter how innocent, would hit his family hardest. He'd promised to divulge everything he knew, including suspects, as soon as he returned.

That hadn't happened and Cal was sure that Gen. Winfield was doubting his own judgment at the moment. The Commandant had enough on his plate. Add to it the guilt of a fallen comrade, in an act that might have been prevented… Cal wouldn't blame Winfield. He'd done what he thought was best at the time. After all, Gen. Ellwood was a decorated Marine, a commander who'd time and time again proven himself on the battlefield.

Cal hadn't known the man personally, but like most Marines in the know, he'd heard of the general's accomplishments.

No, there was more to the suicide than self-pity. Cal wondered how insidious the motive had become in Ellwood's head in order to force the trigger pull. A Marine of that caliber didn't act on a whim.

"That's all we know for now. As long as there's no foul play involved, we may have our investigation wrapped up in a matter of days," said Barrett, closing the file and replacing it in its bin.

Cal was glad for the comment. The last thing they needed was the NCIS snooping around as Cal and his team conducted their own investigation. Gen. Winfield had been very clear on one point, that he wanted Cal's true motive for being in Florida to remain a secret.

Cal agreed. No need to alert anyone until they verified Ellwood's claim. But now they didn't have the Assistant Commandant to help them. What did that mean for the investigation? More importantly, what did that mean for the Marine Corps?

CHAPTER 5

"What the hell is this, Tom?"

Congressman Ezra Matisse (D - New Jersey) was in no mood for games. The Christmas break loomed and the House was still deadlocked on a plethora of items that the stringent Minority leader had planned on putting to rest before they left for the holidays. His phone buzzed for the umpteenth time as he tried to burn holes in the eyes of his fellow Jersey Democrat, Thomas Steiner.

"I think it's a good proposal, Ezra. Just have your staff give it a once-over and let me know what you think," replied Steiner, unperturbed by his peer's outburst.

"I don't have time for this. The president wants the Farm Bill and the Relief Fund shored up by this time next week. If we don't get this—"

"Just look at it, okay?"

"Fine. Just give me the broad brush."

Rep. Tom Steiner shrugged as if it were the most routine of requests.

"It's a proposal to defund the United State Marine Corps."

———

The intern watched his boss talking to Rep. Matisse. Just like Steiner had predicted, Matisse threw his hands up, almost tossing the file in the process, storming off without a word.

Nothing else was needed. The staffer knew what to do. The cell phone already in his hand, he clicked send and a Twitter status update from a fictitious alias floated out into social media.

———

Gregory Garbett was a junior at William and Mary. He'd taken the semester off to intern on Capitol Hill. Like most of his peers, he shared a tiny apartment with five other guys. Not only was it impossible to bring a female friend home, it was also impossible to get the rank smell of that many male bodies out of the stuffy air.

He was the only one at home, a rarity. Usually he'd be at work or in a cafe networking with potential employers, but he'd answered an ad the day before on Craigslist. It was a simple job and paid well. $100 for sitting around wasn't bad. He didn't even make $100 for a whole day of running around kissing an old politician's ass.

The cell phone that had arrived on his doorstep an hour earlier pinged. He looked at the screen and saw the Twitter status update. *Boring*, he thought.

As he picked up the phone that had only one number programmed in its favorites, Gregory wondered if he could get in any trouble for what he was doing. He didn't know who he was doing this for, and what it was he was passing on. They'd promised to send the payment to his PayPal account.

In the end, he shrugged off his unease and dialed the number.

"Hello?" someone answered on the other end.

Gregory looked down at the printout in his hand and read the line that corresponded with the correct Twitter update.

"Yes, I was wondering if you had any jars of pickled eggs."

It sounded ridiculous to Gregory. If this was some spy shit, they needed to get their stuff together. Nobody ever said something that lame in the movies.

The response came a moment later. "I'm sorry. We just sold our last case."

The line went dead, and a second later, so did the phone.

He'd been instructed to throw the phone in a public waste can. Gregory put on his coat and headed for the door. He already knew the bar where he was going to spend his money.

———

Ten similar interactions were made over the next thirty minutes. All innocent. All simple. Should the NSA, CIA or any other agency intercept one of the messages, analysts would surely skip over the innocuous conversations, a handful in a haystack of millions they churned through every day.

The final resting places of the messages took the news stoically. They knew their roles. For the rest of the day, final preparations would be made. Boots tied. Systems re-checked. Weapons cleaned.

———

THE WHITE HOUSE
1:33PM

"Mr. President, you have Congressman Matisse on line one," announced the president's secretary over the intercom.

President Brandon Zimmer looked up from his work.

"Thank you," he said, picking up the handset and pressing the blinking button. "Good afternoon, Ezra." Zimmer liked the bookish New Jersey congressman. A lot of the younger generation didn't. They thought the Jewish politician was too much of a throwback, stoic and diligent, when he should've been fiery in his rhetoric.

During his brief stint in the House, President Zimmer had come to not only respect Matisse, but truly admire the man's legacy. He'd been a member of the House since the early '80s. Even the president's father, the late Senator Richard Zimmer (D-Massachusetts), who leaned conservative more often than not, had said, "If you want to learn how to have a long career in Washington, watch and listen to Ezra Matisse. He'll still be here long after we're dead."

Zimmer had listened to his father, studying the New Jersey Democrat's legislation from over the years. Despite Matisse's natural political leanings, Zimmer found that the Jersey son of a rabbi was pragmatic in his approach, and realistic while others merely sought the praise of their constituency or the glow of the media spotlight. Simply put, President Zimmer held Congressman Matisse in high esteem.

"I'm sorry to bother you, Mr. President. I...well, I thought I should bring something to your attention."

Zimmer couldn't remember the last time he'd heard Matisse so flustered. He waited for his former colleague to continue.

"I wanted you to know before it leaks to the media. Honestly, I don't have a clue why Steiner would do this."

It was like Matisse was talking to himself.

"*Tom* Steiner?" Zimmer asked.

The question seemed to snap Matisse out of his haze.

"What? Oh, yes. Tom Steiner. Sorry, Mr. President. As if I didn't have enough on my plate already."

"Why don't you start at the beginning, Ezra?"

Zimmer heard the congressman grunt and then say, "Mr. President, Congressman Steiner has introduced a bill to disband the United States Marine Corps."

The blunt recital shocked the president. He'd come to know the Marines on a very personal level. General McMillan, the Chairman of the Joint Chiefs, was one of his closest advisors. He'd personally pinned on the new Marine Commandant's insignia at 8ᵗʰ & I. One of his best friends, no, most of his new best friends, men who had risked their own lives to save his, were Marines. Cal Stokes. Daniel Briggs. The massive black former Marine Master Sergeant Willy Trent. What would they think of Steiner's proposal?

He knew what Cal would do if he could: march over to Steiner's office and cold-cock him. Daniel, the strong courageous, shadowy sniper, would be more subtle. Trent, hell, who knew what Top would do?

"And you're sure he's serious?" asked Zimmer, suddenly remembering that he'd recommended Cal to the Commandant at his change of command, something about an internal investigation. The president didn't know the details.

"I'm having my people read through it now, Mr. President. It looks like whoever helped Tom put this together was very thorough."

"Please keep me apprised, and let me know if you need me to step in."

"I hope that won't be necessary, Mr. President, but thank you."

President Zimmer replaced the phone in its cradle and sat back in his chair. Surely there was no merit to Congressman Steiner's plan. Who knew what would happen when the Marines found out? The streets of Washington would be clogged with former Marines demanding that Congress be torn down for incompetence.

Until he heard more from Matisse, Zimmer decided he didn't want to concern Cal. His short-tempered friend would flip his lid and probably hop on the first flight to D.C.

Luckily, he had someone who could help and he was only a few feet away. Earlier that year he'd made one of the smartest moves of his political career. He'd recruited a former Navy SEAL, and former CEO of Stokes Security International (SSI), to be his chief of staff. If anyone knew how to deal with the Steiner situation, it was Travis Haden, Cal Stokes's cousin.

CHAPTER 6

Congressman Antonio "Tony" McKnight (R-Florida) didn't come from money. His father had been a drunk and died serving a life sentence in a backwater Florida prison. His mother…well who knew where she'd ended up. He'd lost track of the woman years ago.

McKnight was a survivor. He'd ascended the political ranking system despite the dead weight of his lost family. A quick learner, McKnight had stepped into the bureaucratic arena like he was slipping into a pair of well-worn house slippers. It was a perfect fit.

He was young, good-looking and single. He surfed the web and scooped up social media followers with ease. There were weeks when a new model clung to his arm daily, and there were others when his relentless work schedule imposed a celibate break for the dashing up-and-comer. *The Washington Post* had recently named him America's Number Two most eligible bachelor, one step behind President Brandon Zimmer.

Nicknamed "The Miami Matador," a nod to his Hispanic heritage and his electorate base, McKnight was becoming known for facing down the onslaught of stalwart old-timers of both parties, much like a matador in the bullring. McKnight had at first laughed at the moniker, but the name and its deeper meaning grew on the social media savvy politician.

He'd taken to re-tweeting photoshopped pictures of his face on some matador's body, usually shirtless. His favorites were the amateur cartoons that cropped up every other week, depicting him in one or another scene where he (as the matador) was taking on some stodgy bill or lumbering curmudgeon in the nation's capital.

Tony McKnight had never been to a bull fight, but his publicist was working on it. It would be a perfect photo op, another notch in his belt. Pictures were the new platform.

As the Hispanic community swelled in America, so did the need for fresh-faced newcomers on the political scene. McKnight was the Right's up-and-coming Hall of Famer. He'd made it to the Majors, but he hadn't cracked into the All-Star game.

It was just a matter of time.

In the beginning, McKnight sought out benefactors, men, and occasionally a woman, who had their own needs. Most were wealthy investors or business owners. In exchange for his ear and a chance on The Hill, they lavished him with trips and donations.

There were legal ways of turning these thinly-veiled bribes into legitimate income. Again, his chameleon-like ability to blend in ensured there would always be a fresh supply of cash. Instead of going to them, donors were now coming to him. It was always satisfying to the man who'd once stood ashamed behind his mother as she handed over food stamps for milk and cereal.

He liked his life. Men of lesser talent and middling ambition might let things ride. That wasn't McKnight's way.

He looked around at his colleagues as they convened for another four hour session. McKnight didn't see competition; he wasn't even in awe of a single one of them. No, what he saw as plain as if it were, in fact, the case, was a herd of cattle, the odd bull mixed in, milling about like placid cows on the plains.

It would soon be time for The Miami Matador to tame them, one by one if he had to. He was smart enough to know that it wouldn't happen overnight. Overt frontal attacks would rarely be the tactic. There were plenty of ways to break a man, to snatch victory from the jaws of defeat.

He smiled, relishing the moment and his hopes for the future. If they were anything like the dreams of his past, he had no doubt that his vision would become a reality.

Not for the first time, McKnight silently addressed his father, who he could only assume now rested in Hell, *I'll be President of the United States in spite of you.*

Rep. Tom Steiner sat down with a smug grin. He'd played second fiddle to Ezra Matisse since his first day in Congress. He replayed the look of shock on Matisse's face after the comment of the Marine Corps's defunding.

"Mind if I scoot by?"

Steiner looked up to see the face of the handsome Floridian, Tony McKnight. He didn't know the man, but he sure knew the upward trajectory of the charismatic new-comer. He hadn't been in Congress a month before he was gracing magazine covers nationwide. Steiner didn't have anything against McKnight, but he wouldn't have minded a sliver of the recognition the Miami native got on a weekly basis.

"Sure," responded Steiner, moving his legs to the side so McKnight could walk by.

"Thanks." McKnight moved by, but then turned around like he'd forgotten something. "You going to the U2 concert tomorrow? I heard you were a fan."

Steiner perked up. The question surprised him. He'd probably never said more than a few words to the younger statesman. But Steiner had been a fan of U2 since their debut record, *Boy*, hit the airwaves in the States in the '80s. He wasn't about to tell McKnight that though, and he was always wary of favors.

"No. Couldn't get tickets," he replied.

McKnight flashed his world-famous smile. "I'll keep my ears open. Maybe some seats will come open."

Steiner nodded as McKnight went on his way. The New Jersey congressman watched McKnight go, wondering what it was like to live a day in the life of a political superstar.

———•———

McKnight waved to friends and enemies alike as he made his way to his seat. He'd never officially met Tom Steiner before, but he knew his type. Steiner was a fringer, always on the out-skirts of the big time. If McKnight was the soon-to-be All Star of the team, Steiner was the sometime reliever that was sent in during throwaway games. His reputation was nonexistent. He could disappear and few would notice.

Every re-election Steiner faced was hard-fought and always contentious. He didn't have the bag of money like McKnight. His donors just wanted to keep a Democrat in office.

But Congressman McKnight had seen the flicker of jealousy in the man's eyes, followed by the "just wait and see" grin. Tony McKnight knew all about Steiner's proposal. Steiner was looking for the big payoff. High risk, high reward. Steiner didn't have a clue. He wasn't even the architect.

McKnight knew the man behind the plan. He was intimately familiar with every word in the soon-to-be public file.

How did he know? Because he, a Republican, a staunch conservative, the youthful face of his party and a likely contender for the next Presidential election, was the man behind the idea, the composer making the music, the plan that would see him ushered straight to the White House.

CHAPTER 7

DISNEY YACHT CLUB RESORT
LAKE BUENA VISTA, FLORIDA
5:29PM, DECEMBER 5TH

Mrs. Ellwood was waiting for them in the lobby. Cal recognized her from the photo Special Agent Barrett had shown him and Daniel. She was beautiful in the old Southern way. Distinguished and almost regal, her silver hair was pulled back in a bun. When she turned, Cal caught of glimpse of the sorrow in her eyes. The look was replaced by the cordial gaze of a professional military wife, a general's wife.

"I'm Cal Stokes, Mrs. Ellwood, and this is Daniel Briggs."

Cassidy Ellwood shook their hands and said, "I've reserved a room where we can talk in private. My family is still in our suite."

They followed General Ellwood's wife down the long nautical-themed hallway. When they reached their destination, Mrs. Ellwood touched the pink band on her wrist to the electronic lock. It flickered green and the three entered.

Mrs. Ellwood flipped on the lights and took the first chair she found in the small sitting area. She motioned for Cal and Daniel to do the same.

Nothing in her appearance, other than the hint of puffiness around her eyes, suggested that she was in mourning. That didn't surprise Cal. Being a Marine wife for as long as she had, surely she'd dealt with her fair share of grief over the past thirty-some years.

Cal began. "I'd first like to say how sorry we are for—"

"For my loss? For the fact that my husband blew his brains out? You can save your words, Mr. Stokes. I'm a big girl. I've seen too many Marines take their lives. I was one of the ones that had to help pick up the pieces for the grieving wives, the widows forced to care for their fatherless children. So spare me the song and dance. What does the Commandant want with me?"

Cal nodded. He hadn't expected the meeting to be easy, but the level of animosity made him pause. "General Winfield wanted me to come down and let you know that he is at your disposal. Anything you need, we will help take care of it."

"What about the Marine Corps? They already sent their delegation."

"This is in addition to that, Ma'am."

Mrs. Ellwood cocked her head to the side taking the two men in. "Who are you, Mr. Stokes? Are you a Marine?"

"Former Marine, yes, Ma'am"

Mrs. Ellwood snorted. "Didn't you hear the last Commandant? There are no *former* Marines. Once a Marine, always a Marine." She spat the words out like they'd burned her mouth.

"Yes, Ma'am. I don't like to confuse people, especially without a regulation hair cut. Daniel and I are no longer on active duty," Cal explained.

"Then what are you doing for Scotty Winfield?" She seemed intrigued now, her anger just below the surface.

"That's a little hard to explain, Mrs. Ellwood."

"Try me. I've been around the block a few times, Marine." She sounded like a general. Patiently tolerant.

Cal couldn't tell her the whole truth, so the Commandant had told him to use his discretion on what he said to Mrs. Ellwood.

"We've been directed to help in the investigation of General Ellwood's death."

"I would think it's pretty cut and dried, gentlemen. My husband told us he would meet us in an hour. Instead he returned to our room, pocketed the pistol my daddy gave him, and walked into the woods to take his own life."

He could see that she was trying to stay strong, but her lips were quivering. Cal made his decision.

"Mrs. Ellwood, we believe, that is, myself and General Winfield, believe that there might be more to your husband's death."

Mrs. Ellwood's eyes went wide.

"You're telling me that not only did the Marine Corps take my husband away from me for decades, but now you're saying that it might have had something to do with his death?" Tears were now streaming from her eyes. She didn't seem to notice. "God damn the Marine Corps! Honor, courage and commitment? What happened to family? We tell our young Marines and their wives to take care of one another, to be there for their children. But that's all a lie! My children never had the benefit of their father's love. He wasn't home. He was supposed to be the example, but Doug was always working. Now my grandchildren will never know their grandfather."

She paused to grab the tissue Daniel had extended to her. Mrs. Ellwood dabbed her eyes and continued.

"I'll tell you something that isn't in your files, Mr. Stokes. We came on this trip because of me, because I demanded it of my husband. I really thought he understood. He took the time with our boys, with their kids. We made love and for a moment I thought I had my Doug back. We were kids again. I loved him very much, Mr. Stokes. I love him…"

Her voice trailed off as she sobbed quietly. Cal stood up from his chair and knelt in front of her, taking her free hand.

"I understand," he said simply.

Mrs. Ellwood's eyes flashed. "How could you?!"

He didn't look away. "My fiancé was murdered in front of me, and my parents were both killed on 9/11."

Her eyes softened and she covered his hand with hers.

"I'm sorry," she said.

"It's okay. I'm very sorry for your loss, Mrs. Ellwood."

She nodded, wiping her tears away with the tissue.

"My husband was a good man, an honest man, Mr. Stokes. He worked hard and did his best. There wasn't a lying bone in his body. But he was a Marine through and through. It was in his blood, I know that."

"He was a Marine's Marine, Ma'am."

Mrs. Ellwood nodded absently. "You were saying…are you telling me that there may have been a reason that Doug did what he did?"

Cal didn't see the harm in telling her something.

"Yes, Ma'am."

She smiled. "For some reason that makes me feel better. Doug wasn't a man who could fall into self-pity. I...I didn't believe it when they told me." Her eyes met Cal's again. "Can you promise me something, Mr. Stokes?"

"If I can, I will."

"If there was someone behind my husband's death, if they did something to force Doug's hand...Find them, Mr. Stokes. Find them."

For some reason, despite the odds stacked against them and the enemy still lurking in the shadows, Cal said the first thing that came from his heart, "We'll take care of it, Ma'am."

CHAPTER 8

The two men dressed as the building's security guards were down the stairs and out the front door exactly three minutes and fifteen seconds before the FBI investigators descended. Warrants were waved and badges flashed as the on-site security team tried to figure out what the agents wanted.

"This federal warrant gives us immediate access to suite 409," said the lead FBI agent, attired in a Bureau windbreaker over his thick winter coat.

"Sir, I'll have to call the building manager first," replied the forty-year-old night watchman. He'd been an employee at the same complex for almost six years, ever since he'd taken early retirement from the Navy. This was the first time he'd personally encountered the FBI. He'd heard stories, but none of them lived up to what was facing him now. The special agents just kept coming through the front doors, some with boxes, others with cameras, and still more with laptop bags slung over their shoulders. "I could get in a lot of trouble if—"

"You'll be in federal prison if you don't escort us up to suite 409. Now, would you rather get stuffed in the back of one of our vans or show us the way?"

The security guard tried, but couldn't match the FBI agent's glare.

"Okay," he replied, already making his way toward the bank of elevators.

The FBI agent snapped his fingers and was instantly followed by his entourage. Twelve of them squeezed into the elevator with the sweating guard. He kept his eyes on the doors, watching the intense reflections of his fellow passengers.

He'd already told them that no one was in the office. He'd even offered to give them the tenant's contact information so that maybe they could come in themselves. But the FBI had its own plan. They wanted in now.

The doors slid open and the security guard was greeted by black clad troops with rifles. He almost pulled out his own weapon, but the large agent stepped around him and said, "They're with us."

How had they gained access without him knowing? His sweat turned cold as he imagined the inevitable conversation he was going to have with his boss. He gulped once and fumbled in his pocket for the key card. After a quick swipe, the door unlocked and he was pushed aside by the armed raid force.

He stepped back and watched as the FBI team swarmed in. No one paid any more attention to him and that was fine with him. He realized he had to go to the bathroom, so he walked to the fourth floor restroom, passing the sign for Suite 409, with its Marine Corps emblazoned sign that read *USMC F-35 Liaison and Procurement.*

He'd met the Marine colonel who commanded the Marine and civilian staff who worked in the office. The guy didn't say much, but to a former squid, the Marine seemed wound pretty tight. That was saying something for a Marine.

The security guard wondered what the colonel was going to do when he came to work and found the FBI waiting. He didn't really care. After taking a leak, it was just another night on an otherwise boring shift.

WASHINGTON, D.C.
11:30PM

The Chairman of the House Armed Services Subcommittee on Seapower and Projection Forces stifled another sneeze. He was coming down with something, probably from one of the grandkids. They been up to visit from Chesapeake the week before, and two of the three hadn't stopped with their runny noses and incessant coughs. He loved the little rug rats, but, man, were they bred to spread whatever the latest crud was.

Rep. Wade Yates (R-Virginia) blew his nose into another tissue and added it to the growing pile in the waste basket sitting next to him.

"Gentlemen and ladies, we've been at it for most of the night, and I'm sure you'd like to get home. May I suggest we adjourn until tomorrow?"

There were no disagreements from the other nineteen members of the subcommittee that provided oversight for Navy and Marine Corps procurement and research and development. Some yawned as they gathered their belongings and said farewell to their peers.

Congressman Yates couldn't remember another December that had been so plagued by budget squabbles and deadlock. Despite President Zimmer's attempts to bring the two sides together, it was the same old story in Washington. Left versus Right with no end in sight.

Yates shook his head as he stuffed the last file into his brief case. There was still much to discuss, but at least the bulk of what they were finalizing was actually cemented in the budget. The F-35 Joint Strike Fighter program had been a particular bear, but they'd gotten through it. With cost increases and delays from the manufacturer, the U.S. government was increasingly in the hole on the expensive program.

Various news outlets had done their best to paint the program as another example of government waste, but Rep. Yates and his colleagues believed in the program. They didn't disagree on revamping the process and holding the manufacturer accountable, but they were steadfast in their insistence that the F-35 was a must-have for the future of the American armed forces. He'd said as much two days before in an interview on *60 Minutes*. They hadn't aired it yet, but he was hoping they'd include the meat of what he'd put forth.

He was the last out the door when his cell phone rang. He debated not answering the call, but saw that it was one of his assistants. Yates answered.

"Shouldn't you be asleep by now? We've got another long day tomorrow."

"Sir, I'm sorry to bother you."

The tone of his staffer's voice wiped the grin off Yates's face.

"It's okay. I was just leaving the subcommittee meeting." He wondered what could be so urgent at this hour. "What's the matter?"

"Sir, I just got a call from the FBI."

Yates stopped walking. "What did they want?" He scoured his mind for any ongoing investigation that he should've remembered. His brain was foggy from the cold, or maybe it was the flu.

"They just raided the Marine's F-35 liaison offices in Dulles, and they've taken Colonel Pearce into custody."

CHAPTER 9

Special Agent Robbie Barrett had a pounding headache and it had nothing to do with overindulging the night before. Although he lived well and liked to enjoy the finer things life had to offer, he maintained certain peculiarities with his work. One of his steadfast rules was that he never touched alcohol while on a high-profile case.

The death of the Assistant Commandant of the Marine Corps was a tragedy, but it was also an opportunity for Robbie Barrett.

He'd spent the evening before with a young woman his mother had introduced him to at a family event at the Barrett home in Orlando. She was cute enough and plenty smart, but his mind couldn't focus on the conversation.

He could tell she thought he was off cue for not even taking a sip of the eighty-dollar bottle of wine he'd ordered, but she didn't say anything. He'd deposited her back at her brand new apartment, and barely gave her a peck on cheek before he was speeding away back to his home office.

And there he'd stayed until well past three in the morning. The case was as plain as any he'd seen. A guy has a shitty day, or maybe even a shitty life, and he decides to end it all. Nothing new in Barrett's world. He'd investigated possible murders and countless suicides in military barracks, rundown motels and even the one time he'd had to pick through a pile of stinking red snapper to get to the body covered underneath.

As he walked another loop around the scene of Gen. Ellwood's ultimate demise, Barrett wondered if he was looking because there was actually something there or because he wanted something to be there.

If there was another angle, some conspiracy that the Marine general had wriggled his way into, that could mean lots of media exposure. That could thrust him into the spotlight, a proposition that made him more than a little excited. Maybe if his mother and father finally saw that he was doing something important, something that could garner the attention of the public, then maybe, just maybe, they'd stop pestering him about using his law degree for something useful.

They hadn't understood his decision to leave his father's firm and enlist with NCIS. That's what they'd called it: "enlisting," as if either of them had the faintest idea what military service meant. He hadn't known much when he'd started, but he learned quickly, busted his ass to prove he belonged amidst the ranks of former-military.

So while his parents schmoozed their friends and whispered their hopes that someday Robbie would "get over his service and come back to the family," he spent his days doing what he could to rise through the ranks at NCIS.

He knew that the other NCIS agents called him names behind his back, *Pretty Boy, College Boy, Trust Fund*...but he ignored them. The Barrett family's fuel was success, and Robbie Barrett had stuffed handfuls of it in his pockets as his colleagues watched, mouths watering. They could say whatever they wanted, but it didn't change the fact that he was fast becoming the face of the NCIS in Florida.

Only half paying attention to his surroundings, he back-pedaled to get a better look at the crime scene. His heel caught on a something hard and Barrett felt his momentum propelling him back, arms already moving to stop the fall. Before he hit the ground, something grabbed him, arresting the wipeout.

"Gotcha," came a voice.

Much less gracefully than he would've liked, Barrett regained his footing and whipped around, his hand searching for his firearm.

He stopped when he recognized the man standing before him, blond hair pulled tight in a ponytail. If he was amused, he didn't show it. Daniel Briggs stood with a look that bordered somewhere between curiosity and determination. Barrett could feel the man's eyes taking him in, as if he were assessing the NCIS agent's worth.

"What are you doing here?" Barrett asked, a bit of a quiver in his voice that he tried to cover with a cough.

"I thought I'd take a look around," said Briggs, bending down to examine something on the ground.

"Where's Stokes?"

If Barrett was being honest with himself, he would have admitted that the two Marines unnerved him. It wasn't the fact that they'd been sent by the Commandant, or even that they were treading on his turf (he dealt with Washington outsiders on an all-too-frequent basis). It was the way they carried themselves, especially this Briggs character. He had the look of a man who'd seen things, done things. Like a poet who'd finally found his harmony with the world, Daniel Briggs exuded something that Barrett wished for daily: tranquility.

"Cal's seeing what he can do to help Mrs. Ellwood and the family," said Daniel, not looking up as he moved to another spot a few feet away.

"You know we've been over the area a hundred times," said Barrett, seeking to regain the upper hand.

"I know. Not trying to step on any toes. Just thought I'd soak it in without anyone being here."

At that moment Barrett realized that the Marine had probably been there much longer than he had. What had he seen? What was he looking for? But rather than snap a reply, Barrett's mind wondered if his hunch had been right, if there was something more to the case than a run-of-the-mill suicide.

"You have much experience with this?" he asked, following Briggs's path.

"You mean crime scenes?"

"Suicide."

Briggs looked up. "Yeah."

"Personally or professionally?"

"Both."

There was something in the comment and the tone that subtly told Barrett to back off.

"You don't say much, do you?"

Briggs shrugged and continued his inspection of the area.

"How far out did your teams look?" Briggs asked.

"A couple hundred yards. Figured there wasn't much need considering the circumstances."

Briggs nodded.

"Hey, if there's something I need to know, it sure as hell would be helpful to have it before I file my initial report," said Barrett, matching Briggs's pace as he moved farther into the brush.

"I want to show you something."

Open space turned to tangle, and then back again. While Barrett swatted away branches, Briggs seemed to melt in and out of the landscape. His footsteps were light, his gaze moving like a predator's.

They reached a small rise and climbed it, the pine needles under their feet still wet from the morning dew. Briggs turned around when they reached the top.

"Look," he said, pointing back the way they'd come.

Barrett did as he was told, squinting, and then taking off his suddenly fogged sunglasses to see what Briggs was pointing at. It took him a moment, but then his eyes went wide. They were probably half a mile away, but there, clear as day, was the yellow taped crime scene, his Escalade parked just where he'd left it.

"How did you know this was here?" asked Barrett, the possibilities already tumbling around in his head.

"I had a hunch."

Briggs walked over to a clump of trees, his eyes taking in the area. He went to his knees, and then down to his hands.

Barrett watched as he maneuvered around the small copse that looked more like a nest on the ground, probably big enough to be home to a deer. It dawned on the special agent what he was seeing. This wasn't a private refuge for animals, it was—

The loud crack of splintering wood overhead made him look up in confusion. He saw the shattered remains of the tree branch not a foot above his head. It took a split second for him to realize what it was. Just as he did, the wind was knocked from his chest as Daniel Briggs tackled him and the pair rolled down the backside of the hillock. Over and over they went, pitching over prickly palmettos and narrowly missing saplings as they rumbled end over end.

They finally came to rest with a splash in a knee high body of water. Briggs had a pistol out. He put his index finger to his lips and motioned for Barrett to follow.

Embarrassed by his slow reactions, Barrett slid his own sopping wet weapon out of its holster and tried to pretend he knew what was going on. He'd never been shot at before. He'd never pulled his service pistol in the line of duty.

"What's happening?" he whispered, trying to calm his breathing.

Another crack overhead. This time Barrett realized it was a high-caliber round, a rifle most likely. He ducked involuntarily, but Briggs just kept moving. If he was worried, he didn't show it.

"Who knew you were out here?" asked Briggs, his voice flat.

"What? I…I don't know. Why?" stuttered Barrett, the edge of panic in his brain crept down his arms.

Briggs shook his head. "Never mind. How well can you swim?"

"What?"

"How well can you swim?"

It was then that Barrett noticed they were up to their chests in the murky water.

"I can take care of myself."

Briggs nodded and pulled off his shirt with a swift tug. "Strip down if you need to. We're going that way." He pointed deeper into the gloom where trees hung over the waterway with their drooping tendrils, roots visible as they formed skeletal cages against the banks.

Barrett debated kicking off his shoes but thought better of it. As he gulped at the thought of gators and whatever else lurked below the surface, he followed Briggs, hoping they'd make it out before a bullet found them and left them for the swamps.

CHAPTER 10

CAMP LEJEUNE, NORTH CAROLINA
7:47AM, DECEMBER 6TH

The Commandant of the Marine Corps waved goodbye to the formation of men outside 3rd Battalion 2nd Marines's headquarters. They'd invited him for morning PT, and although he was three times the age of some of them, he could still more than hold his own. There was something about being with a Marine infantry battalion that got his blood flowing, reminded him of what it was all about.

He needed that on this day more than ever. The infantry Marine, grunt, knuckle-dragger, ground-pounder, was the core. Every other specialty, from supply to intelligence, supported the infantry. Even Recon Marines and their elite brothers in Force Recon were technically tasked with supporting the lowly grunt. It was the way it had always been.

As an infantry officer in his earlier twenties, Winfield had the privilege of leading Marines from every walk of life. They came in all shapes and sizes. Sometimes they were such a challenge that you wanted to wring their necks, but in the end they were family. You took care of family.

As his driver pulled away from 3/2's pavilion, Gen. Winfield reflected on his new mission. He was somehow supposed to save the Marine Corps from the worst fate imaginable: extinction. And with what? A handful of trusted advisors and a former staff sergeant.

While he didn't doubt Stokes's abilities (he had come recommended from none other than President Zimmer himself), he was beginning to see the tidal wave forming on the horizon.

First came the tremors, the warning from Gen. Ellwood. Then came the rumble, Gen. Ellwood's death. And just this morning he'd found out about the FBI raid on the Marine offices in Dulles. The head of the liaison section, Col. Pearce, was now in for questioning.

He'd fielded thirteen phone calls from politicians on both sides of the aisle, some wanting answers and some looking for blood. It felt like the enemy was coming from all sides, attacking in the dead of night, and then slinking back into the mist.

What he needed more than ever was a shred of hope, a clue as to where the next attack would come. It wasn't like he could close ranks and tell his Marines to seek cover and be at the ready. No, this was a nefarious foe who'd already shown a penchant for surprise.

His mind wandered as he gazed out the window, Marines going about their morning routines as they had for hundreds of years. What would they think if they knew what they were up against?

They passed by a set of pull-ups bars. The sight of a Marine attempting to do a one-armed pull-up reminded him of an old friend, one of his mentors who'd taught a bitter young Marine captain what the Marine Corps should be.

He pulled out his military ID card from his wind-breaker pocket. It was wrapped in a rubber band. Winfield flipped it over and pulled a frayed laminated yellow card out from behind his ID.

The card had a faded note on the front next to the FMF-PAC (Fleet Marine Forces Pacific) Command logo. It said, "Keep that candle high and you'll always have your troops with you."

Below the logo was a simple title: *Band of Brothers*. The card's content had been written long before the popularity of the *Band of Brothers* book or movie. It was penned from a military hospital in 1951 by a wounded Marine second lieutenant who'd just been told his wife had given birth to a healthy baby boy. It had started out as a letter to his newborn son, sort of a "this is how to live your life" thing that a father should pass on to his children, especially his firstborn son.

But the birth wasn't the only reason the lieutenant wrote it. He'd also been told that he would be forever paralyzed from the waist down, never to walk again. His Marine Corps career was over.

And so he'd written the letter to his son, trying to imagine what life would be like without his beloved Corps, without the ability to walk like a man, like a warrior. Something about the simple act of writing emboldened him; it made him realize that the fight was not yet lost. The thought of seeing his son only heightened his resolve.

He wrote his rules to live by and secretly enlisted the aid of his hospital ward compatriots. The mission was simple: he would walk again.

And walk he did.

Despite the intelligence and prognoses of a dozen doctors, that Marine lieutenant shuffled to the hospital door with a box of cigars in hand, shouted the announcement about the birth of his son down the hallway as he tossed the cigars in the air, and then passed out cold.

When he came to, the lieutenant was surrounded by medical staff demanding to know how he'd done it, how he'd walked despite his seemingly irreparable spinal injuries.

He would go on to win the Silver Star for his exploits in Korea, and would serve thirty-five years in his beloved Corps.

Captain Winfield had met LtGen. C. G. Cooper when he was at a crossroads in his own career. He was bitter about where his tour was headed, and the caliber of Marine officers in general.

Gen. Cooper had seen the pain on his disgruntled face. He'd requested to see Winfield and they'd taken a long walk along the coast of Kaneohe Bay. The general didn't say much, he mostly listened. He trudged along asking questions, and for some reason, Winfield poured out his guts.

When they finally reached a point overlooking a beautiful slice of the shining Pacific, Gen. Cooper reached into his pocket and pulled out a yellow card. He told Winfield the story about how it came to be, and the solemn promise he'd made to God should he be allowed to walk again. "I told God that I would spend the rest of my life giving our young Marines the kind of leadership they needed and deserved. You're part of that legacy, Scott."

Gen. Winfield, now the Commandant of the Marine Corps, wondered what his now-deceased former commander would say if he knew what Winfield was facing. He knew what the Mississippi general would say. He'd tell him to keep his candle lit and live by the words on that tattered card.

Winfield smiled and read it:

<u>BAND OF BROTHERS</u>

1. ALL MARINES ARE ENTITLED TO DIGNITY AND RESPECT AS INDIVIDUALS, BUT MUST ABIDE BY COMMON STANDARDS ESTABLISHED BY PROPER AUTHORITY.

2. A MARINE SHOULD NEVER LIE, CHEAT, OR STEAL FROM A FELLOW MARINE OR FAIL TO COME TO HIS AID IN A TIME OF NEED.

3. ALL MARINES SHOULD CONTRIBUTE 100% OF THEIR ABILITIES TO THE UNIT'S MISSION. ANY LESS EFFORT BY AN INDIVIDUAL PASSES THE BUCK TO SOMEONE ELSE.

4. A UNIT, REGARDLESS OF SIZE, IS A DISCIPLINED FAMILY STRUCTURE, WITH SIMILAR RELATIONSHIPS BASED ON MUTUAL RESPECT AMONG MEMBERS.

5. IT IS ESSENTIAL THAT ISSUES AND PROBLEMS WHICH TEND TO LESSEN A UNIT'S EFFECTIVENESS BE ADDRESSED AND RESOLVED.

6. A BLENDING OF SEPARATE CULTURES, VARYING EDUCATIONAL LEVELS, AND DIFFERENT SOCIAL BACKGROUNDS IS POSSIBLE IN AN UNSELFISH ATMOSPHERE OF COMMON GOALS, ASPIRATIONS, AND MUTUAL UNDERSTANDING.

7. **Being the best requires common effort, hard work, and teamwork. Nothing worthwhile comes easy.**

8. **Every Marine deserves job satisfaction, equal consideration and recognition of his accomplishments.**

9. **Knowing your fellow Marine well enables you to learn to look at things "through his eyes," as well as your own.**

10. **Issues detracting from the efficiency and sense of well-being of an individual should be surfaced and weighed against the impact on the unit as a whole.**

11. **It must be recognized that a brotherhood concept depends on all members "belonging"—being fully accepted by others within.**

The Commandant closed his eyes and said a silent prayer of thanks. He knew the coming battle wouldn't be easy, but he once more had his resolve, and possibly the answer.

CHAPTER 11

Cal was just leaving. He'd spent the last two hours trying to help the Ellwood family in any way he could. It turned out that the best thing he could do was entertain the kids as the adults went about their duties. The little girl, Lily, had taken an instant liking to him, saying, "Up, up, Cow," every time he put her down.

The adults had finished their packing with drawn faces and puffy eyes. More than once Cal felt their stare on the back of his head. He knew the healing would take time, and judging by the tone of Gen. Ellwood's sons' voices, they were far from understanding what their father had done.

Cal sat down and waited for the bus that would take him to Downtown Disney. From there he would walk to the Hilton where he and Daniel were staying. They were supposed to be calling the Commandant at noon. He hadn't heard from Daniel since he'd left earlier that morning, but that wasn't unusual for the sniper.

The bushes behind the bench rustled. He turned to see what animal was there, but was surprised to find Daniel's face instead. Cal noticed faint traces of mud along the sniper's jawline, like he'd tried to clean off his face but missed a few remnants.

"What are you doing back there?"

"We've got a problem," said Daniel. His calm face was a stark contradiction to the comment.

"What happened?" Cal asked, rising to join his friend. He took in the rest of Daniel's appearance. His jeans were scuffed and wet at the ankles. They moved deeper into the tree line, Daniel not answering the question.

They came upon a man sitting on the ground, his head between his legs. He was rocking slowly and looked up when he heard the two Marines approaching.

Cal scowled. The man looked ten times worse than Daniel. His preppy clothes were soaked through and there were multiple tears on both his paisley shirt and his tailored pants. It took a moment for Cal to recognize the guy. It was that NCIS agent. Cal frowned.

"What the hell is he doing here?" Cal asked.

"They tried to kill us," blurted Special Agent Barrett, wiping a droplet of blood from the gash on his forehead.

Cal looked at Daniel. "What's he talking about?"

"My hunch was right," replied Daniel.

"What hunch?"

Daniel shrugged. "I told you I was going back to take a look at the crime scene."

"And?"

"I found a sniper's nest."

"What? You never said anything to me."

"I didn't want to get your hopes up."

Cal shook his head, trying to come to grips with what his friend was saying.

"Are you telling me that General Ellwood was shot by a sniper?"

"No way," interrupted Barrett. "The ballistics all came back positive for a self-inflicted wound."

Daniel nodded in agreement. "I'm not saying that anyone else took the shot."

Cal exhale almost came out in a huff. "So what are you saying? How do you even know it was a sniper's nest?"

He knew it was a stupid question as soon as it left his mouth. Daniel wasn't just any Marine sniper. He was *the* Marine sniper. Cal had never seen or heard of anyone better.

"First, from the faint markings and general settling in the area, I'm eighty percent sure whoever was in that nest was there when General Ellwood pulled the trigger. Second, whoever it was, and it was one man without a spotter, he knew what he was doing."

"You didn't say anything to me about that!" said Barrett. "Are you telling me that there's a sniper running around Orlando?"

Daniel cocked his head, regarding the disheveled NCIS investigator. "Who else did you think was shooting at us?"

Barrett's mouth dropped open.

"Hold on. You're telling me that a sniper took the time to infiltrate the area, setup a perch, watch the general shoot himself, and now he's dumb enough to come back and shoot at you guys?" Cal shook his head. "It doesn't fit, Daniel. Why would he do that?"

"I'm not sure. Maybe he left something. Maybe he was checking in on the investigation. Who knows."

Cal tried to imagine what might possess a professional to risk detection by revisiting the location he'd successfully exfiltrated. It didn't make any sense.

"Okay. Let's assume it was the same guy. Let's assume that he's just dumb enough to snoop around again. Why was he there in the first place? Why didn't he kill Ellwood himself?"

Daniel crossed his arms over his chest and said, "Because he was only there to make sure General Ellwood took his own life."

———

The sniper cursed as he watched the smoke from the small fire he'd lit at his former hide. He'd misjudged the Commandant's emissaries.

If it hadn't been for that Boy Scout troop who'd literally almost tripped over him the morning of Ellwood's suicide, he wouldn't have even considered coming back. He heard them before Ellwood took the shot, and assumed incorrectly that they'd take a more circuitous route, or even run away from the gunfire. Instead they'd found the highest point they could. That spot happened to be right where he was gathering his gear and preparing to leave.

The six Boy Scouts and the parents hadn't seen him. He was too good for that. But in his rush he hadn't had time to fully cover his tracks. That had necessitated the return trip. If he hadn't it would have nagged at his fastidious brain for months.

What he hadn't counted on was Daniel Briggs making his own visit. The sniper had hoped that Briggs had already had his fill of the scene. Briggs and Stokes were reportedly booked on a three o'clock flight back to Virginia. But once again all his planning was for naught.

Luckily, his rifle was in the trunk of his car. He'd stalked his prey and whomever the companion was. His shot was ready, crosshairs leveled. But at the last moment he'd recognized the other man. It made the sniper hesitate. Killing Briggs and stashing the body was one thing, but getting the NCIS even more involved could mean real trouble, trouble he and his employer didn't need. His hesitation not only cost him the killing blow, it also complicated the situation. They'd gotten away, somehow disappeared. He didn't dare chase them down. Not now. It would have been too risky.

But his employer would understand. He knew the uncertainties of the battlefield and the fog of war whose untimely presence rarely failed to make itself known.

He smiled as he put his car in drive and pulled out onto the dirt access road. If he and his employer could make a Marine three-star general take his own life, it would be easy to take care of Daniel Briggs and Special Agent Barrett.

CHAPTER 12

The Christmas decorations adorning every nook in the White House were extravagant as ever. A pile of holly here and an enormous handmade wreath laced with silver and gold threads there. Some days the scent of cinnamon or peppermint wafted in from some hidden location. Today it was the smell of fresh pine needles. It reminded President Zimmer of family holidays in the mountains, something his U.S. Senator father always insisted on, despite whatever crisis gripped Washington.

The White House staff continued to set the bar for contemporary yet tasteful decor. To Zimmer it felt like they'd somehow tailored it to the tastes of their president, even though he hadn't lifted a finger to help. As he half-listened to a former colleague from the House, he realized that they'd placed little mementos like the painting of a snow-covered wood cabin in the hall, the requisite tail of smoke rising from its chimney into the still sky. It looked remarkably like one he'd stayed in during his teenage years. They'd done that for him, taken his childhood memories and crafted the holiday to his image. He'd have to remember to thank them personally. It touched him that they would go to such extremes.

"Well, Mike, it sounds like you've got your hands full. Please let me know how things turn out," said Zimmer. The congressman took the hint and moved on to find another ear for his pet project.

The brunch had been a success. It was small compared to others they'd hosted since he'd taken the oath of office, but this one was of his own design. He'd wanted to say thanks to those who'd help craft his administration amidst the ever-shifting sands of the world stage.

At the top of his list was his chief of staff, Travis Haden. He'd almost had to beg to get the former SEAL to agree to come to Washington, but Cal's cousin had performed like Zimmer knew he would. Precise. Task driven. Firm but fair.

They'd learned a lot from each other and their friendship had grown. Zimmer was happy that he'd been able to thank him in front of career politicians.

There were others, like Rep. Ezra Matisse (D-New Jersey), who'd helped spread the president's message through the Democratic party in the House. Vice President Milton Southgate, a one-time rival who'd almost derailed Zimmer's presidency, had probably been the second most helpful, after Travis. It always amazed the president to see what the simple arch of an eyebrow or waggle of a finger from Southgate could do to get the train back on the line.

It had surprised none in his party to find out that fully half of the twenty men and women who'd been invited to the thank-you brunch were from the Republican Party and the military. The two highlights from those camps being Congressman Tony McKnight and General McMillan, the Chairman of the Joint Chiefs.

Zimmer knew that he might face McKnight in the coming presidential election, but the Florida Republican had been honest and fair. He'd helped Zimmer at a particularly hard time earlier that year when it seemed that the entire world was out to torpedo the White House.

The president chuckled when he looked across the room to where Gen. McMillan was telling some story to three Democrats. He could tell they were out of their league, but they listened all the same. Zimmer admired McMillan like one might love a cherished uncle. He was always there with calming, sage advice. No challenge was insurmountable to the Marine general.

Zimmer took a sip of his Mimosa and wished he could've invited Cal and the rest of The Jefferson Group. They, above all others, were the reason he was still in the White House, and more importantly, why he was still alive. But the only people in the room that knew a thing about Cal's covert charter were Travis Haden and Gen. McMillan. Cal and his team didn't want or necessarily need the public thanks, but it would have been nice anyway.

His reverie was interrupted when Rep. McKnight stepped up next to him and offered his own glass in toast. "To a wonderful way to start the holidays, Mr. President."

They clinked glasses and each took a drink.

"I meant what I said, Tony. We couldn't have done what we did this year without your help."

The handsome Floridian smiled. "You may be wanting to take that back come election time."

Zimmer laughed. "How about we just agree that if it ends up being the two of us in the general election, we'll try to keep things above the belt?"

"I'll drink to that, Mr. President." McKnight finished his drink and grabbed another from the table. "I was wondering if you had a second for me to bend your ear.

"Sure. I think I've got ten minutes until my entourage drags me out of here kicking and screaming."

McKnight nodded, his face suddenly grim. "Mr. President, I wanted to know how you're handling the Marine Corps situation."

"And which situation would that be, Tony?" Zimmer somehow kept the smile on his face. According to Gen. Winfield, the Marine Corps was doing everything it could to keep a lid on the Assistant Commandant's death, at least until they could find out more. As for the matter of the bill proposed by that crazy Tom Steiner, Ezra Matisse had informed the president just before the luncheon that he believed the proposal would be laughed out of Congress. There were just too many military veterans serving on both sides of the aisle now. The ongoing wars since 9/11 had seen to that.

"I'm not sure if you've heard, but I just got word that the Assistant Commandant of the Marine Corps, General Ellwood, committed suicide while on vacation with his family," said McKnight.

Zimmer motioned for McKnight to follow him farther into a corner.

"Where did you get your information, Tony?"

"I have friends in Florida law enforcement. They knew I could be trusted with it."

The president tried to remain calm, but his insides were boiling. "If this gets out before we know for sure—"

Congressman McKnight put up his hand to interrupt the Commander in Chief. "That's not why I brought it up, Mr. President. I did only so that you would know that I want to help. This won't stay secret for long, and if someone like Tom Steiner gets his hands on it—"

"So you heard about that, too?" Could anything be kept under wraps on The Hill?

"I have, and it's ridiculous. Trust me, I'll do everything I can to get it thrown out. Steiner will look like an idiot."

Zimmer didn't know how to respond, and that fact bothered him. He was a career politician, used to wheeling and dealing with every side. Here was another example of a situation that not only slammed into him after a successful pow-wow, but had the potential to make one of the country's finest assets, the United States Marine Corps, look bad in the eyes of the country.

"Thanks for the heads-up, Tony. I'll let you know what we find out."

"I would appreciate that, sir. I'd hate to see anything bad happen to the Corps."

Zimmer nodded, suddenly tired. He had to find Travis and tell him the news. His chief of staff might know what to do. They should probably tell Gen. McMillan, who could relay it to Gen. Winfield. Zimmer's mind spun as he started stacking up the to-do list in his head. One thing that crisis after crisis did was condition a brain to compartmentalize and look at things from an objective angle.

But there would be much to do, on top of everything they were trying to accomplish with the federal budget. To make matters worse, there was one thing he dreaded doing most: putting in the call to his friend, Cal Stokes.

CHAPTER 13

The Jefferson Group leadership (minus Cal and Daniel), sat around the conference room table in the secure War Room. They'd just ended their phone call with Cal, who'd given them the latest on the situation in Florida and the conversation he'd had with the president concerning Congressman McKnight's untimely revelations.

"What can we do to get ahead of this thing?" asked Jonas Layton, CEO of The Jefferson Group (TJG). He'd made billions in the tech world but now served as the face of TJG. He was the newest arrival. The rest of the group had worked together for years. It hadn't taken him long to fit in, since being a near genius with the talent for foreseeing future events lent itself well to what they did.

"I've got my bots trolling, but other than the little that's been reported in the news, they've found zilch so far," said Neil Patel, twirling a mini-screwdriver in his hand that he'd just been using to tinker with a pile of metal pieces sitting in front of him. Neil was a genius and had made millions for Stokes Security International with his inventions. There wasn't a week that went by that he didn't hand a new toy to one of his friends to play with.

"I say me and Top jump in the jet and give Cal and Snake Eyes some backup," said Gaucho, a stocky Hispanic whose braided beard nearly hung down to the table. "He's gonna need every shooter we've got."

The Jefferson Group had anywhere between fifteen and twenty operators on-hand at any one time. They were a seasoned team of elite warriors, tested in battle and loyal to their team and their country.

"I know you can't wait to jump in our shiny new plane again, but why don't we wait and see what Cal needs," suggested Master Sergeant Willy Trent, USMC, his near seven foot dark frame towering over his best friend. "Something tells me we're gonna be useful up here before long."

Gaucho's jaw clenched, but he didn't disagree. The former Delta soldier huffed in frustration.

"Doctor Higgins, what do we know about this Steiner guy?" asked Jonas, jotting something down in his ever-present journal.

The Jefferson Group's resident shrink, and former CIA head interrogator, shifted in his seat. "Representative Thomas Steiner. Second ranking Democrat from New Jersey. Unremarkable life other than his time in Congress. Has had a run-in or two with the law, nothing serious. Both charges dropped. Lives alone. Works most days."

"Do you think it would be useful to put him under surveillance?" Jonas asked, still taking notes.

"I would think that the question might be better answered by one of my colleagues here with experience in the field, but since you're asking, I would suggest starting with something passive, say using Neil's talents?"

Higgins was alluding to Neil's uncanny ability to hack into anything with an electronic pulse. No one in the room could remember a time when the Indian born computer geek had been stumped.

"That shouldn't be a problem," replied Neil, adjusting his new grey and black speckled Cartier eyeglasses. "Anyone else you want me to snoop on?"

"Let's start there. I'm sure there'll be more soon," said Jonas. "Now unless you guys have anything else?"

No one did, and they adjourned to their respective tasks. The men of The Jefferson Group didn't need handholding. They each had their place and worked like a mechanism specially made for tackling impossible missions. As the tech side went about their duties on the computers in the War Room, MSgt Trent and Gaucho headed to the kitchen.

"What are you making for lunch?" asked Gaucho, his stomach rumbling.

"How's peanut butter and jelly sound?"

Gaucho rolled his eyes. Trent was a classically trained chef. His mouthwatering meals were another bonus for the men working at TJG. Every Sunday the entire team gathered in the main house for a family style dinner cooked by Trent.

"Okay. You want me to make quesadillas instead?"

Gaucho's head bobbed eagerly even though Trent had said it as a joke.

Before the huge Marine could whip out another comeback aimed at his friend's ethnicity, the doorbell rang.

"I'll get it," said Trent. "You go get the tortillas ready."

Again Gaucho didn't catch the joke, and rushed off into the kitchen. Trent shook his head with a rumbling chuckle.

The doorbell rang again. Trent looked through the small peephole and grinned. He opened the door with a flourish, bowing at the waist.

"Good day, milady. To what do we owe this pleasure?"

Diane Mayer's smile was strained. Trent caught the look on the pretty U.Va fourth year's face.

"Is everything okay, honey?" he asked.

"I know Cal's not here, but I thought I might come talk to you guys anyway."

Diane and Cal had been dating for a few months, something MSgt Trent and the others were more than happy about. Not only was Diane a great gal, able to put up with the constant ribbing between Cal and his friends, but she'd brought peace back into the broken-hearted Marine's life. After losing his fiancé, they'd worried that Cal might never find true happiness again. Trent was pretty sure Diane was the one.

She wasn't supposed to know what Cal and his team officially did for a living, but Trent was pretty sure she did. Neil had found out that prior to enrolling at the University of Virginia on an ROTC scholarship, the blonde co-ed had served one enlistment with Naval Intelligence. He'd never voiced his opinion to Cal, but the crusty master sergeant figured it was only a matter of time before they let her in on their little secret.

"Come on in. I was about to fix some lunch. Want some?"

Diane shook her head. "Is there somewhere we can talk?"

Trent realized that this was the first time she'd been in the house/headquarters. Cal spent most nights at her place when he was in town.

"Sure."

Trent led her inside and turned into the small parlor that sat just inside the front door. He closed the French doors and they both took a seat.

Diane took a deep breath, and then said, "I know I'm not supposed to know what you guys do around here, and I'm not going to ask. Cal's probably going to kill me when he finds out I came."

"Why don't you just tell me what's wrong. I'm sure he won't mind. If he gets out of line, I'll smack him around a little."

Diane looked up and smiled. "Promise?"

Trent drew a cross over his heart and put three fingers in the air. "Scout's honor."

"Okay. You know I was in the Navy, but do you know what I really did?"

Trent would've preferred she not ask the question, knowing that she would assume that Cal had been spying on her. But it looked like the cat was out of the bag anyway.

"Intel," he said.

She didn't look surprised. "I assume you know how I feel about Cal too."

"You two are pretty close."

Trent wondered where the line of questioning was going.

"I love him, Willy," she blurted. "I would do anything to keep him safe. But I know I won't always be able to do that. He's his own man. Stubborn and proud, but I love him." She looked at her hands and went on. "I still have friends in the intelligence business. I won't tell you where because it doesn't matter. When Cal came back from his trip overseas, you remember, right after we started dating?"

Trent remembered. Cal had led the hand-picked international coalition that drove the stake into the heart of ISIS. He'd been wounded in the process. Nothing major, but impossible to hide from Diane.

"I do remember."

"Well, I reached out to two of my old friends and asked them to…I don't know how to say this without sounding like a stalker…but I asked them to keep an ear out for the name Cal Stokes. Now, before you say anything, there's not surveillance or anything like that. It's more like a Google alert. If something came across their desk through various intel gathering networks, they promised to let me know."

Trent cringed inside. Diane was right. Cal wouldn't be happy. He'd consider it an invasion of his privacy instead of what it really was: someone who loved him watching out for him.

Diane went on. "Yesterday I got a call."

"And?"

"We met for breakfast. I had to drive up to Warrenton to meet him. I can't tell you who he's with, but he said that in the last two days there've been repeated mentions of Cal."

"From who?"

"He couldn't say."

"Couldn't or wouldn't?"

"I think couldn't. He did say that he thinks it's someone in government based on certain systematic indicators."

Trent nodded. "What was the context of the conversations?"

Diane reached in to her purse and pulled out a thin stack of folded paper. "The transcripts are right there. I'll leave them with you."

Trent took the stack and asked, "Diane, what do they say?"

The composure she'd been trying so hard to maintain left her, tears streaming from her eyes as she said, "They want him dead, Willy. They want to kill Cal."

CHAPTER 14

Rear Admiral Joseph Gower nodded to the Jamaican customs agent who looked as bored as anyone he'd ever encountered. It made him wonder how diligent their screening process really was. Then again, who was trying to bring illegal substances *into* Jamaica?

He grabbed his civilian passport from the counter and made his way to the Sandals Lounge. A bubbly concierge named Martha greeted him and ushered him inside where she said he could have his pick of complimentary snacks, soda or Red Stripe beer on tap. He would've loved a flimsy plastic cup of beer, but he opted for a bottle of water instead.

Five minutes later, his date arrived, taking in the lounge like a child seeing Mickey Mouse for the first time.

"It's so pretty!" she exclaimed as she set her carry-on bag next to him and kissed him on the cheek. "I won't even ask what you paid for all this."

Gower shrugged as if it didn't matter and that nothing was too good for her. In fact, he hadn't plunked down a nickel for the trip. The man he was supposed to be meeting had insisted he come.

The Navy admiral had at first refused, citing work as an excuse, when in reality he really just couldn't picture himself on the impoverished island. Although he didn't come from money, Gower appreciated the things that money bought. He believed America was a shining example of that fact. Go to most U.S. metropolitan areas and you'd find clean streets and a safe place to live and work. It was one of the reasons he'd gone into the service, to preserve that way of life.

He had friends who paid ungodly amounts of money to visit places like Africa, Haiti and Vietnam. Gower had always preferred to stay in the continental U.S., enjoying the luxuries his service to his country had bought.

But then he'd mentioned the proposed trip to his current girlfriend Nancy, a fifty-year-old administrative assistant who worked at the Pentagon. She was attracted to his position and he, well, he was attracted to the prospect of an occasional roll in the hay. The trip was all Nancy had talked about for the last week. He was sure it would lead to much hay-rolling.

Their names were called and a porter led them out to a waiting oversized van as he pushed a cart overflowing with luggage. Once he'd ensured his own bags were tucked neatly in the back of the vehicle, Gower boarded the mini-bus that was thankfully blasting cold air from overhead vents. He sat down next to Nancy, who was gabbing away with another middle-aged woman a row back. He smiled and tried to seem sociable, but was glad when they started moving as it turned Nancy back to the task at hand.

Her hand rested on his leg and he briefly imagined her topless.

"Aren't you excited, Joe? I swear if I hadn't stopped by the ladies' room that I might just pee in my pants."

"I'm glad you like it," he said. "Only the best for you."

She kissed him on the cheek and then turned to look out the window with wonder. Gower imagined what she must be seeing. All he could take in was the contrast to the U.S. It reminded him of the couple times he'd visited Tijuana as a brand new Navy ensign. Trash littered the streets and natives just seemed to be hanging out for no better reason than they had no other place to be. There were even multiple signs advertising personal security services as they drove away from the airport. What did that say for the state of the small island nation? Gower was glad they'd soon be ensconced in an all-inclusive resort.

An hour later, they were over halfway to their destination in Ocho Rios. The driver asked his passengers whether they'd like to stop to use restrooms up ahead.

"Discovery Bay is just up the hill," he announced. "It is where Christopher Columbus first discovered Jamaica."

There were impressed murmurs from some of the other passengers, but Gower wanted to roll his eyes. He resisted the urge and raised his hand instead.

"I wouldn't mind stopping for a quick bathroom break," he said.

There was a barely concealed groan from someone in the back, but he ignored it.

The request didn't dampen the driver's spirits. "All good, mon. One minute."

Two minutes later, Gower stepped off the bus and made a bee-line for the restroom. After relieving himself, he took a circuitous route back to his ride and found a spot overlooking Discovery Bay. It was nothing too impressive in his opinion. They'd made sort of an open-air museum in tribute to Columbus's landing, complete with a replica wooden ship's bow that allowed visitors to take in the view of the bay below.

He made his way there and was soon joined by another man who seemed consumed with taking pictures of the vista.

Without stopping what he was doing, the man said, "Look on the ground against the wooden railing."

Gower did as instructed and found a small brown paper shopping bag. He picked it up and inspected the contents. There were a couple Jamaican baubles along with two bottles of water and an envelope.

He looked up from his perusal, but the man with the camera had already moved on. Gower ripped open the sealed envelope and smiled at the stack of traveler's checks. Under the money were instructions for the next day's meeting. While he understood the need for the secrecy, he wondered if his host was taking things too far.

Gower wouldn't question it though. The thousands in his hands were tiny crumbs compared to where things were headed. If his new friend wanted to play spy, so be it. As long as he kept his promises, the career Navy man would go along. After all, what were a few harmless games and a trip overseas compared to millions flowing into your bank account?

CHAPTER 15

Diane Mayer lay curled in a ball, the shivers refusing to release their hold on her prostrate form. Occasionally another tear trickled down her cheek and onto the pillow. Even exhaustion couldn't send her to soothing sleep. Worry kept her going.

Cal was late. He was never late. Not once in the months they'd been together had he failed to show up on time. It was one of a million reasons she loved him, why she couldn't go fifteen minutes without thinking of him. It was so against everything she'd prepared her life for. She had one semester left in school and then it was off to serve her country once again, this time as a Naval officer.

Years of planning and preparation had been swept away by one man, the man that she couldn't see herself living without. They were like two forces of nature that tried everything they could to stay apart, but somehow kept getting pulled back together.

Her friends thought he was a little stiff at times, but she understood where the hesitation came from. He was cautious with strangers, showing just enough emotion to be cordial. Despite her Naval intelligence background, Diane was the exact opposite. Since arriving at U.Va, she'd cast off her prior distrust and embraced the community of bright and enthusiastic young men and women. There weren't many places she could go without seeing a friend.

Cal, on the other hand, had a small group of loyal friends for whom he would do anything. He guarded them even though they didn't need guarding. They were his family. It was yet another reason she loved him and couldn't live without him.

He challenged her. She challenged him.

But now Diane wondered if she'd gone too far. After revealing what she knew to MSgt Trent, she'd only gotten one phone call from Cal. He'd been brief, almost curt. "I'll be in town tomorrow. When can I stop by to talk?"

She'd told him that all her semester finals would be done by 3:30pm and that she could be back at her apartment by four.

"I'll see you then," he'd said, and then the line clicked off.

That was the night before. It had taken every ounce of self-control she had to a) make it through her last two exams, and b) not pick up the phone and call him.

Conclusions banged around in her weary head as she waited. *He doesn't want me anymore. I crossed the line. He'll never trust me again. I love him. I lost him.*

As another tear slipped down, Diane heard a key being inserted into her apartment door. She sat up and tried to compose herself. *I must look like a basket case*, she thought.

Cal stepped in the door and locked it behind him. He didn't say a word, quietly removing his jacket and hanging it on the coat rack next to the door. In the dim light his face looked drawn in shadow. She couldn't read him in that moment. What was it in his stare? Anger? Sadness? Disgust?

"Hey," he finally said, still not moving from where he stood.

Diane hugged the pillow tight against her chest as if pushing the word from her diaphragm.

"Hey," she answered.

"Have you eaten yet?"

"No. You?"

He shook his head. Still he stayed where he was. Her stomach turned. She wanted to run to him, throw her arms around him and never let go. But she resisted, waiting to see what, if anything, he would say.

"I don't know what to say." The words slipped from his mouth and entered her heart like a poison dagger. This was it.

"It's okay. I understand," said Diane.

He looked confused. "What?"

"I said I understand. I understand why you have to...why you have to say what you have to say."

Still the look of confusion in his eyes, those eyes...

Cal took a hesitant step forward.

"Diane, I—"

"It's okay. I shouldn't have done what I did. Don't worry, I'll be okay."

Another step forward and she could see him better, his eyes soft, wondering.

"Wait, did you think...did you think I was coming here to break up with you?"

"Aren't you?" the words came out in a sob.

Suddenly, he rushed forward and enveloped her in his arms. All the waiting, all the worrying, it all converged as the emotions burst forth and Diane allowed herself to be consumed.

She didn't know how long they sat there, saying nothing, his arms never budging from their protective embrace. The beat of his heart against hers. His steady breathing. She couldn't find the courage to look at him, keeping her face nestled against his chest.

If this was going to be the last memory she had with him, Diane prayed it would last forever.

"I'm sorry," he said.

She didn't reply.

"Top told me you stopped by the house."

Her body tensed involuntarily. Here it was. The axe to cleave them apart.

"Uh huh," she muttered.

"That's why I came by as soon as we landed."

Diane sucked in a huge breath and pushed herself back. If he was going to do this she would have the courage to look him in the eye.

"I shouldn't have—"

He silenced her by putting a finger to her lips.

"Let me explain," he said, adjusting his position on the bed. "You don't know how many times I came to see you with the plan all laid out."

"What plan?"

Cal looked away. "I'm no good for you, Diane."

Her hand reached up to his cheek and turned his face back to hers.

"You are perfect for me."

His eyes hardened, again the resolve. "No. You don't know what I do. It's no life for someone with your potential. You have so much to give, and I'm...well, I'm..."

"You're mine," she said softly.

"That little scratch I got was nothing, Diane. I could disappear and you'd never see me again. You don't deserve that. You should be with some hotshot lawyer who'll take you to Bora Bora."

The absurd comment made her burst out laughing. She couldn't control it, eyes closed, head thrown back as the ridiculousness of the situation bubbled over.

"I don't see what's so funny," he said, his tone with that edge that she usually heard when he was on one of his rare anti-politician rants.

Finally the laughs and giggles subsided and she could look at him again.

"We are both complete and total idiots, Cal Stokes."

His eyebrows shot up at the comment.

"What are you...?"

"Just shut up and listen to me." She laughed again. "I love you, Cal Stokes. Do you think I'd go into something as huge as love without doing a little homework? I don't know exactly what you do for a living, Cal, but I sure as hell know it isn't wining and dining as a consultant."

"But I—"

"I told you to shut up!"

She was overjoyed to see him smile, that mischievous grin that came out when they were alone. He put his hands up in surrender.

"Thank you," she said. "Do you think I'm the first woman to fall in love with someone in your line of work? I know the risks. I know it won't be easy. We'll have crappy days and unexpected absences. But I don't care. I want to be with you, despite the risks, despite the sacrifice. I've lived the last eight years thinking I knew what I wanted. And then one day you step into my life like the stubborn Marine you are, and I'll be damned if you're not the only thing I want. I'm sorry that I kept tabs on you, but I love you, Cal. I worry about you. Not in a crazy stalker way, but from the beating heart of a woman who loves her man. I would do anything for you. It's not conventional and it's not convenient, but that's not who I am and neither are you. So you can tell me to butt out and mind my own business, and that's fine. But just know that as long as you'll have me, I'll be here, for you, for me, for us. Always."

She looked up at him, wishing he'd say something, anything. Again the look that she couldn't identify. Then she noticed the corner of his mouth twitching like he was trying to keep his mouth closed. He pointed to his mouth as if to say, "Can I speak now?"

Diane rolled her eyes and nodded.

He let out a chestful of air along with a chuckle.

"Feel better?" he asked.

"I do. You?"

"Yeah. Look, you know my history, or at least most of it. You know about Jessica…"

Diane had read all about Cal's murdered fiancé after he'd told her about the brazen attack.

"I'll admit, I was mad when Top told me about the transcripts you gave him. I'm sorry. It's who I am. I'm not used to people checking up on me. But Top can be pretty persuasive."

"What did he say?" Diane asked.

"I think his exact words were, 'If you give Diane shit about this, I'll rip your arms off.'"

"He said that?"

Cal nodded. "He must really like you. Maybe you should be dating him."

Diane slapped Cal playfully on the leg.

"Ouch."

"Stop crying, Marine. Tell me the rest."

Cal rubbed his leg like he'd been wounded. "Well, after he told me that, and Daniel told me pretty much the same thing, I took a walk and thought about things."

"Like what?"

"I don't know. Life. You. Me. The thing is, Diane, I love what I do. It's part of who I am. Sure I've got my bad days, but I get to go to work and really make a difference. Do you understand what that feels like, why that's so important?"

Diane nodded.

"So I started thinking about how I could have it all, a life and my passion." Cal's voice drifted off with his thoughts.

"And?"

"I made a phone call."

"To who?"

"My boss."

"Jonas?"

Diane had spent plenty of time with Jonas Layton, The Jefferson Group's CEO. She'd been just as impressed with his down-to-earth attitude as she had been with the vast wealth he'd built.

"No."

Diane's face scrunched in confusion. "If not Jonas, then who?"

"The president."

"The president of...?" Diane knew Cal did some work for U.Va, had even given a few guest lectures. Was he talking about the president of the university?

Cal's eyebrow rose, indicating that she should guess again. Then it hit her.

"You mean Zimmer?" she blurted. Diane knew Cal was friends with President Brandon Zimmer, but she had assumed that the friendship was based on the fact that Cal's cousin, Travis Haden, was Zimmer's chief of staff.

"At least I'm happy that Miss Smarty Pants didn't figure that one out on her own."

Diane didn't immediately reply. She'd known almost from the start that Cal was into something below the radar, possibly working for the CIA, but if he worked directly for the president, what could that mean?

"What did he say?"

"He said that if you're smart enough to find information that even *we* couldn't get our hands on, that maybe we should be asking you for help."

"He really said that?"

"He did."

"What else did he say?"

Cal scratched his head, and then said, as embarrassed as Diane had ever seen him, "He said that I better pull my head out of my ass and tell you how I feel about you."

"And how do you—"

"Despite all the crap we're probably about to go through, despite my baggage and your nosy habits, I love you, Diane Mayer. I love you."

CHAPTER 16

MARINE CORPS WAR MEMORIAL
ARLINGTON, VIRGINIA
8:30PM, DECEMBER 7TH

The wind whipped the illuminated American flag in a steady flap. Murmurs from the gathered reporters died down as On-Air lights blinked to life across the line of mounted television cameras. Luckily the night was unseasonably warm or else it might've been unbearable.

No one knew why they'd been summoned. What they did know was that the calls hadn't just come from Headquarters Marine Corps, but from the White House as well. Strings had been pulled and the live feed would be fed into homes across the nation in this prime time slot.

At precisely the appointed time, the Commandant of the Marine Corps stepped out from the shadows followed by none other than President Zimmer himself. Reporters swiveled in their seats as still cameras clicked and video whirred.

General Winfield was attired in his blues, an impressive array of medals adorning his left breast along with his leather Sam Brown belt. He looked every bit the Marine. Tall. Weathered in a battle-hardened way. Resolute.

The president took a position just behind the Commandant as Gen. Winfield stepped up to the simple podium. No one in attendance missed the significance of the leader of the free world choosing to stay in the camera shot, ostensibly taking the role of protector and supporter. Journalists nudged their neighbors and scribbled furious notes.

"Ladies and gentlemen, thank you for coming. I won't keep you long, I promise."

Winfield shifted his gaze from those in attendance to the bank of television cameras.

"Since 1775, the United States Marine Corps has served as this nation's expeditionary force in readiness. We've fought in places like Belleau Wood, Iwo Jima, Korea, and Iraq. Like our brethren in our sister services, we've shed blood across the globe in order to protect the lives of Americans and uphold the interests of this nation."

"We have solemnly sworn to protect and defend the Constitution of the United States, against all enemies foreign and domestic, and that we will bear true faith and allegiance to the same. And now, as the world steps back from a wartime footing, we find that our allegiance, our very existence, is being questioned.

"In the coming days you will undoubtedly hear reports that will cause shock and dismay. Some may be true, while others may not be. Reports will surface condemning the Marine Corps, attempting to put us down, to strike enough fear in your hearts that you'll begin to question whether America does indeed require the future service of the United States Marine Corps. What I will promise you now, right here, under the gaze of one of our most sacred monuments, is that the Marine Corps will cooperate in any way we can. Even as I speak, orders are being disseminated to Marine commands around the globe to cooperate with federal investigators, should the need arise. We will not run, and we will not hide. It's not what we do. We will tackle this challenge like we've tackled so many in our rich history, with honor, courage, and commitment to this great nation.

"To the vast majority of Marines, active and retired, I tell you that you have done nothing wrong. For those who have, justice will be swift. As for the rest of you, know that your chain of command has complete faith in your abilities. Together we will see this through.

"To those individuals rallying to Congressmen Thomas Steiner's cry, who believe that the Marine Corps is just another line item on the federal budget, and that we should be replaced by a leaner, but less mean model, I caution you to reconsider. Ask your constituents. See if the American people still want us on that wall, whether they sleep better at night knowing that Marines are protecting their freedom, keeping the wolves at bay.

"To our sister services, I will say that we have worked together for hundreds of years. If the last decade has taught us anything, it's that we each have our own unique role in the U.S. military. We've become closer through training, joint commands and on the battlefield. To put aside those bonds in the name of fiscal responsibility or inter-service rivalry would be a disservice to our country."

The Commandant's eyes went cold as he gripped the top of the podium with his white gloved hands.

"To the forces who may be planning to do harm to my Marines, and who have already been party to the death of the Assistant Commandant of the Marine Corps, General Douglas Ellwood, I am here to tell you that I will fight until my last breath to see you pulled from the shadows. If there's anyone you want, it's me. If you're looking for a fight, you've got one. If you don't have the courage to fight in the open, I suggest you stay in your holes. Either way, I am here, waiting. Don't make me wait too long. Marines aren't known for their patience."

Congressman Tony McKnight traced his lower lip with the rocks glass half full of Grey Goose. He'd been at dinner when one of his aides informed him of the press conference. That text was followed shortly by another text from President Zimmer telling him to tune in. Ten minutes later, he was alone in his study watching the brief broadcast.

Bold move, Mr. President, he thought, sipping his drink.

He'd expected the Marine Corps to keep things quiet. Instead, they'd decided, or rather Gen. Winfield had decided, to confront the threat head-on. McKnight respected the Marine for his bravery, for standing up when waiting for the die to be cast might've been easier, but it was too late.

While he appreciated the sacrifice of the Marines, he wasn't above using them for his own means. And without knowing it, Zimmer and Winfield had played right into his hand. The president didn't have a clue. He'd just tied himself to a sinking ship on national television. He'd basically said that no matter what surfaced concerning the Marines, he, President Brandon Zimmer, supported them fully.

McKnight laughed. The pieces were already in play. All he had to do now was see how many more ropes he could wrap around the president's ankles and wrists as he was dragged into the underwater abyss by his proud Marines. McKnight couldn't wait to see it happen.

———————

CHARLOTTESVILLE, VIRGINIA

Cal answered the call before the first ring finished.

"Stokes here, sir."

"Did you watch?" asked the Commandant.

"Yes, sir."

"What did you think?"

Cal hesitated. Like the rest of America, he'd only found out about the press conference minutes before it began. Dread crept up his back as he'd listened to Winfield's words, especially when he'd mentioned Gen. Ellwood. The Commandant had chucked their plan without even consulting him.

"I'm not sure it was the best move, sir."

"Oh?"

"We may have lost the element of surprise. They know that we know."

Winfield chuckled. Cal bit back his annoyance.

"Sir, is there something I should know?"

"I would've thought it was obvious, Cal. I just did you a favor."

"I'm not sure I understand, sir."

"First, I'm done hiding. I'm going to tackle this thing head on. I owe that to Doug Ellwood and to my Marines. Second, the favor I just did you was to paint a big fat target on myself. I'm sure the rats will start coming out of the woodwork with a vengeance now."

"Where does that leave us, General? We had some good leads, but now…"

"While these bastards get busy tearing me apart, I want you to sneak into the shadows and find the sons-of-bitches."

A diversion. Cal smiled at the thought. Winfield was right. Overt masking covert. The Commandant's admission of fault would be seen as an act of preservation, the final defense. But Cal knew as well as Winfield that sometimes the best defense was a strong, yet silent, offense. Sappers slipping out of the barbed wire line to infiltrate the enemy CP even while the enemy was on the attack. A perfect mission for Cal's team. He smiled.

"We'll take care of it, sir."

CHAPTER 17

SANDALS GRAND RIVIERA RESORT
OCHO RIOS, JAMAICA
9:49PM, DECEMBER 7TH

Rear Admiral Joseph Gower stepped out of the butler driven golf cart on shaky legs. He nodded absently to the driver who wasted no time in speeding off into the night.

Gower took a moment to calm his breathing. It had nothing to do with the ride up from the beachfront side of the all-inclusive resort, where he'd left Nancy at the Promenade Bar on the far side of the wooden pier. It had everything to do with the news conference he'd happened to see as they made their way downstairs for sushi at *Soy* restaurant.

He'd tried to appear nonchalant as he told his date to go ahead and get them a table, but he walked stiffly to the television mounted near the lobby bar. The Commandant's speech was halfway through by the time he could get the damn bartender to turn up the volume, but he got the gist.

After doing everything he could to expedite their dinner, including inhaling the food he had absolutely no appetite for, he excused himself and went back up to their fifth floor room. There he'd watched and re-watched the press conference on his laptop.

Media outlets were already batting the warning shot back and forth, trying to get further information out of the White House and the Marine Corps.

He hadn't expected the brash move from the Marines. Gower had spent decades under the ocean, fighting the silent war with the Russians and the Chinese. It was a chess match of epic proportion, and he'd found as a young skipper that he had a knack for it.

But now the Marines were calling him out. He should have known. Gower tried to call his friend Gen. Mason, but all he got was his voicemail.

So as he shook out his arms and took another breath, he started up the lit trail that wove between butler villas under the tropical foliage. He wondered what his host would be thinking.

Gower knocked on the appropriate door and waited. The walk had given him a chance to regain his footing and piece together a plan.

A moment later, a pudgy man with a disheveled combover and a mussed button down answered the door.

"Admiral! How are you? Come on in. Can I get you a drink? Whiskey? Champagne?"

Glen Whitworth was a fourth generation industrialist whose family's international conglomerate started out building barges during the First World War, but now built everything from fighter jets to submarines. He'd inherited the company two years before when his father had died of a massive stroke in a company board meeting. While Gower couldn't really relate to the younger Whitworth's brash style, he could respect the man for what he'd done since his father's death. He was ambitious in a way that reminded Gower of Teddy Roosevelt. A bull in a china shop. Nothing would stop Glen Whitworth, and he had the bragging rights to prove it.

"No, I'm fine, thank you," answered Gower, needing a drink then more than ever.

"That's right, I almost forgot you're a teetotaler. I apologize. Didn't mean to be insensitive."

Gower almost cringed at the powerful fumes coming out of Whitworth's mouth. He wondered how long the billionaire had been at the sauce.

"It's fine, Mr. Whitworth." Gower's bout with alcohol had almost derailed his perfectly crafted career, hitting an apex when he'd solicited a junior officer's wife in the presence of the Chief of Naval Operations himself. It was one of the few regrets in his life, but he'd abstained ever since, simply utilizing his willpower.

"Please, call me Glen. After all, pretty soon you will be my right hand man."

Whitworth clapped the admiral on the back and slipped over to the fully stocked bar to get a refill.

Gower couldn't take the suspense, so he asked, "Did you happen to catch the Commandant's press conference?"

"I did," replied Whitworth without looking up from where he was filling an entire water glass with dark brown liquid. "I don't see why it should concern us."

Gower wanted to disagree and list off all the reasons he feared the repercussions. But he reminded himself that he was Whitworth's equal, his soon to be the hand-picked CEO of OrionTech. Whitworth wanted to play more of the lobbyist role and hobnob with politicians and military leaders. He'd said the daily running of the company was something he loathed. Gower was more than happy to slide in and take the helm.

"There could be complications."

Whitworth took a healthy swallow from his drink and pointed at Gower. "I thought you told me everything was taken care of. I think you said, and I quote, 'Nothing short of a nuclear holocaust could stop this deal from happening.' Did I get that right?"

Gower colored. "We made certain assumptions, and based on those assumptions the probability of success was determined be close to one hundred percent."

"Don't give me that bullshit, Admiral. You promised me a deal. If you can't deliver, I'm sure I can find someone else who can."

Gower didn't like being threatened. He was the one who called others to the carpet. "Now Mr. Whitworth, I am a man of my word, and when I say something—"

"When you say something to me, it better be the truth." The rage in his eyes subsided and his smile returned. "Now, if we're finished snapping at each other like old women, why don't we sit down and I'll tell you why the Commandant's threat is an inconsequential blip on our radar screen."

Gower nodded and realized he was parched. What he wouldn't give for a glass of whatever his soon-to-be-boss was having. Instead, he grabbed a bottle of water from the fridge, and sat down to listen to what Whitworth had to say.

CHAPTER 18

Congressman Tom Steiner couldn't remember a time when the committee chambers had been filled to capacity. The Committee on Oversight and Government Reform wasn't the sexiest of congressional subsets. The committee's work was often seen more like an Internal Affairs division of a police department than what it really was, a group of politicians dedicated to cutting fraud and waste in the United States government.

But today the committee was making headlines. Crowds loitered outside, each representing their chosen side. There was the Marine contingent. To Steiner they looked like a bunch of worn out has-beens. Camo-wearing Harley riders with chest-length gray beards.

The other side was less represented but equally vocal. They were the crowd that Steiner could relate to. Liberal to a fault. If there was a cause to fight for they were there. Not for the first time, Steiner wondered how so many protesters could drop whatever they were doing and march on the capital. Didn't they have jobs?

Steiner swept the thought away as he reviewed his notes for the fourth time. He tried to ignore the cameras in the gallery, but his heart beat a little bit faster knowing that he would soon be on the grand stage. The spotlight would be his alone.

There had been the heated exchanges with his colleagues and the endless ringing of phones manned by his understaffed team, but he saw it as necessary payment for the final reward. After all, was it smooth sailing for brave men like Dr. Martin Luther King, Jr. or Mahatma Gandhi? They'd believed in their quest for justice, a higher calling. Then again, each of their lives had been taken by a bullet.

Steiner shivered and made a mental note to ask for more personal security for the foreseeable future. Who knew what the Marines would do once the death nail slammed home. You could never trust those PTSD crazies.

The committee chairman's gavel tapped twice. When the talking continued, the gavel pounded in the stout chairman's hand.

"Order, please," he said, glaring at the crowd, his eyes finally resting on Tom Steiner. Steiner ignored him. He'd gotten an earful from his colleague the day before. The old coot would be eating his own words soon enough.

"Now, a few ground rules considering today's showing," said the chairman. "We will have an orderly hearing. If I have to silence anyone in the gallery more than once, they will be escorted from the premises."

There were murmurs of assent from the room and everyone settled in for the show.

"Before we begin, I would like to thank General Winfield and his staff for joining us today." He nodded to the Commandant who sat flanked by his team. Winfield returned the gesture, his gaze unwavering. Steiner wondered what the man was thinking. He'd probably prepared all sorts of lies to cover his own ass. The New Jersey native couldn't wait to put the jarhead in his place.

Winfield was sworn in and the other committee particulars were checked off before the chairman said, "I'd like to say for the record, that I have personally reviewed Mr. Steiner's brief, and despite the allegations, I fully support the United States Marine Corps." There were shouts of approval from the gallery that the chairman chose to ignore.

He allowed the next ranking members to speak briefly. Each said much the same.

Cowards, thought Steiner. The farce went on for another ten minutes. Through it all Gen. Winfield's face did not change.

Finally, the chairman said with a sneer, "The chairman recognizes the representative from New Jersey, Mr. Steiner."

Steiner adjusted his microphone. "Thank you, Mr. Chairman." He sifted through his thoughts and decided to jump right in, the words of a charismatic opening having slipped from his mind. "General, you've been called before our committee this morning to answer our questions. Are you prepared to do so in a manner befitting your rank and station?"

"I already swore an oath, Congressman," replied Winfield.

"But do you promise to give the whole truth and nothing but?"

"I believe I just answered that question, Mr. Steiner."

The two men glared at each other. Steiner wanted to break the arrogant soldier. Didn't he know that he served at the pleasure of the men and women sitting before him?

"Very well. I assume you have had time to review my brief?"

"We only received it last night, but yes."

"And what is your opinion of its contents?"

"Mr. Steiner, this is your show. If there's a question you'd like to ask me, I'm happy to answer it."

Steiner gripped the underside of the desk.

"For the sake of those in the gallery and at home, this brief," he held up the stack of papers, "contains allegations and evidence that the Marine Corps, its officers and its enlisted men, have not only besmirched their once proud name, but they have also tarnished the very visage of these United States of America."

There was more than one groan from the audience and possibly from one of his fellow committee members. He ignored it and went on.

"I will now quote from this committee's mission statement. *We exist to secure two fundamental principles. First, Americans have a right to know that the money Washington takes from them is well-spent. And second, Americans deserve an efficient, effective government that works for them. Our duty on the Oversight and Government Reform Committee is to protect these rights. Our solemn responsibility is to hold the government accountable to taxpayers, because taxpayers have a right to know what they get from their government. We will work tirelessly, in partnership with citizen-watchdogs, to deliver the facts to the American people and bring genuine reform to the federal bureaucracy. This is the mission of the Oversight and Government Reform Committee.*"

He paused, looked around the hushed room, and then began again.

"I believe that the American taxpayer has the right to know what the Marine Corps has done to break the trust with the citizens of this fine land. Fraud. Waste. Bribery. Lack of combat effectiveness…to name a few. Is this what America deserves? Is this what we're paying for? In my humble opinion, the investment of the American people would best be served by another."

The shouts began before he finished his last sentence. House security staff looked to the chairman, who glared at Steiner with cold fury. Steiner's gaze swept over the gallery, coming to rest on Winfield. If the Marine general was overwhelmed with any of the emotion exhibited by the rest of the room he didn't show it. He sat as still as a statue.

Finally another gavel smacked against the wood podium. It wasn't the chairman but one of the newest members of the committee, one of the few Republicans who hadn't said a thing in the beginning, Congressman Tony McKnight.

The room quieted as McKnight spoke. "I'm sure America appreciates your theatrics, Mr. Steiner, but General Winfield came here to answer your questions, not to be chastised like a child. And may I just say for the record, that myself and several of my colleagues tried to dissuade the general from coming. It is my opinion that the contents of this brief, if you can even call it that, are nothing but a litany of lies concocted by individuals and organizations seeking their own betterment. You mention certain high level officials, but never once do you call them by name. Why is that, Mr. Steiner?"

Steiner had expected the question and answered truthfully. "Many of the sources listed are currently on active duty and were solicited for their opinion in exchange for their anonymity. They saw it as their patriotic duty to cooperate and contribute to the study."

"I'm sure they did," replied McKnight.

"I resent the tone of your—"

"And I resent the fact that you can sit here and point the finger at a decorated war hero, a man who has done more for this country than you could ever do, Mr. Steiner. General Winfield and his Marines are a band of brothers entrusted with our safe-keeping. They live by the tenets of honor, courage and commitment. Now, if you could please tell me and the American people why in God's name we should continue to watch this show of yours?"

Steiner smiled. He looked out over the crowd that seemed like it wanted to jump over the barriers and pound him into the ground. Their hate only fueled him. He imagined the magazine covers and countless interviews. That would make up for the hate.

He swiveled his eyes back to the video camera he knew was now broadcasting around the world.

"I'll tell the American people why I called today's hearing. Beyond the fraud and waste, beyond the disobedience and straight up bending of laws, I have one overriding reason for calling today's gathering." The room sucked in a collective breath. Steiner's eyes narrowed and shifted to meet the unwavering glare of the Marine Commandant. "You are no longer needed, General. Your Marine Corps has become obsolete."

CHAPTER 19

Lance Corporal Reece Hock, USMC, wished that every day in the Corps was like this one. As the new guy, he usually got the dog watch. Night time in the Stan still freaked him out. It reminded him of nights in the Arizona desert with his brothers. They used to sneak out of the house and go coyote hunting. It was a stupid thing to do when he was only twelve, but he wanted to be with his older siblings. They were always doing crazy things. Their dad, a former Army soldier with the 101st, just told them to use muzzle awareness and keep each other safe.

In Arizona, it was the sound of coyotes that kept him from sleeping. In Afghanistan it was everything else. Tracers. Mortar rounds. Random shrieks in the darkness. Even though the official war had ended, there was still plenty of fighting going on. His friends at home hadn't believed him when he'd told them.

Hock rolled up his sleeves so he could soak in a bit of the welcome sunshine. That was another thing that had surprised

102

him, the cold. Winter was still winter, another reason taking the late watch sucked a big green weenie. At least during the day you might get some extra temp with the sun.

He heard footsteps behind him and saw one of the civilians who had recently been attached to his Air Naval Gunfire Liaison Company (ANGLICO) team walking up the small rise to the sandbagged lookout post. The guy was fully native, his beard cascading down his chest. He'd introduced himself as Dan. No last name. Even though the guy looked like a tribal elder, Hock's gunny said that the guy was probably either CIA or some former Delta finishing his career with a civilian mercenary company.

They'd first kept him at arm's length, but Dan had proved he not only understood their mission and could call in close air support like the gunny, but he knew the area like he'd lived there for years. He even volunteered to stand watch with the Marines, something he was just showing up to do, if a little late.

Dan took a seat next to Lcpl Hock and extended a can of Skoal. Hock nodded his thanks and grabbed the can, pinching out a bit and sticking it behind his lower lip.

"Seen any good movies lately?" Dan asked, slipping the Skoal back under his muddy robes.

"I saw *Act of Valor* on our way over. You know, the one about the SEALs?"

Dan spit on the ground. "SEALs."

Hock couldn't see behind Dan's black sunglasses, but he detected more than a little of the intra-service rivalry in the man's tone. Hock and his team had worked with the SEALs on more than one occasion. While a couple of them were cocky pricks, most of them were good dudes. One of the senior chiefs had even given him a free pair of boots. They were a lot better than the crap the Corps issued you.

Before he could come up with a response, Dan shifted and grabbed the binoculars resting on a small wooden platform.

"What is it?" asked Hock, straining to see what had gotten Dan's attention.

"Holy shit. Take a look."

Dan handed the binoculars to Hock, who did a quick scan of the area. Nothing. He turned back to Dan. "I don't see—"

The rest of his words came out in a gurgle, the pressure of the blade piercing the surprised Marine's throat, reaching for his spine.

Dan watched him with uncaring eyes as he casually pushed the two foot blade farther until Hock was pinned against the sandbag wall. The thrashing didn't last long. Dan waited. He looked at his watch and then pulled out a cell phone and typed in a quick text.

He pulled off his bloody gloves and tucked them under the dead Marine. Next he took out a remote charge and set it against the mounted fifty cal machine gun.

Two minutes later, he passed through the makeshift OP gate and promised to be back before sunset. Five minutes after that, the first rounds landed, 80mm mortars. That lasted ten minutes as the Marines tried in vain to hail higher headquarters on the radio. Dan had taken care of that, too. When the enemy force appeared in front of Lcpl Hock's post, someone tried to man the machine gun, but it was quickly silenced by the push of a button. Four Marines died in that explosion alone.

It took another twenty minutes for the one hundred Pakistani fighters to overwhelm the ten remaining Marines.

Dan had to give it to the dead bastards. They'd lasted ten minutes longer than he'd predicted.

He pulled out his cell phone and sent off another message. After the text went through, Dan uncovered the motorcycle he'd stashed in a shallow cave days before. The engine started instantly. The sun was dipping over the horizon. Perfect time to leave.

It was time to disappear for a while. His had been the first shot fired. His brothers would take care of the rest. He sped off into the dusk without another thought about the dead Marines whose bodies were now being picked over by the dirty Pakistanis.

Over the next three hours, two Marine companies, one in Iraq and one in Afghanistan, and five teams embedded with local troops from Ghana to Indonesia, perished as if they'd been plucked from the earth. There were no calls on the radio, no warnings of an imminent threat. With overwhelming force the killing happened, as if the very assets once under Marine control had suddenly turned on their masters. Bombs crashed and artillery exploded, leaving Marine blood spilled and soaking into the soil. It wouldn't be until the next morning that their remains were found and the fingers started pointing.

CHAPTER 20

Congressman Tom Steiner was having the time of his life. The early wake up call was a small price to pay for the roller coaster he was captaining at the moment. The first interview had gone live just after 6:30am. His newly hired publicist had scheduled the easiest first. The questions were softballs lobbed in between friendly banter. The NPR host was a known liberal with a penchant for criticizing the military in his weekly *Wall Street Journal* column.

It was a good warmup for Steiner, who'd had few occasions to sit on the world stage in previous years. His feisty publicist was with him every step of the way, hounding stylists like a drill sergeant. She gave him a rating of four out of ten on his first go-around.

"You looked nervous, unsure of yourself. If you want to hit this thing out of the park you need to grow a pair, Congressman."

He was only shocked for a moment by her straight forward style. Steiner reminded himself that she was a pro. She'd revived the careers of half a dozen washed up Hollywood actors and her fair share of politicians. He knew of two in particular who'd revived their political aspirations because of the publicist's Nazi-like precision. She wasn't cheap, but she was worth it.

By the third interview at *The Morning Show*, she rated him at a seven and a half out of ten.

He was now sitting across from two hosts at CNN, who were questioning him about his Marine Corps study. Steiner felt like his fourth interview was going swimmingly. He could get used to the routine of it.

"Congressman, tell us how you intend to sell your proposal to the American people. You must know that veterans are already up in arms about this."

Steiner nodded with a grave smile. "This has nothing to do with the contributions of the Marines. This is a simply being fiscally responsible. The last time I checked, it was the American people who demanded we politicians fix the economy, balance the budget and weed out the waste. I heard them loud and clear when a month ago the American people overwhelmingly voted for a Republican held Senate and House. Some of my good friends lost posts they'd held for close to two decades. Well, I'm taking the mandate very seriously. So when I was approached about this problem, we took a serious look at it. Remember, this is not personal. This is business. Americans have said that they want the government to run more efficiently, to learn the lesson of corporations like General Electric, Apple and Starbucks. I'm in complete agreement. Just like these corporations, we need to make cuts, get leaner, and come up with better, more efficient ways of doing business. If people have a problem with targeting the Marine Corps, I'm sorry, but as I've already said, they have identified themselves as the most easily replaced service in—"

There was a commotion behind the cameras and then both hosts pressed fingers to their earpieces. The male host kept his composure, but the woman's face blanched.

"Like I was saying…" Steiner tried to continue, imagining what his publicist would want him to do.

The male host put up a hand. What were they doing? The cameras were still rolling. Steiner shifted in his seat and placed his hands in his lap.

Finally, the male host spoke, his voice thin and emotionless. "I'm sorry, Congressman. We've just received word that multiple Marine units serving overseas have been attacked. There are numerous casualties. Our producers are working to get more information. We're going to cut to a commercial and be back in a minute."

The LIVE sign went out and everyone scattered, leaving Steiner by himself. His publicist was by his side in seconds.

"What happened?" he asked.

She sat down next to him. "It looks like hundreds of Marines have been killed."

Steiner's face went gray. "How? What happened?"

The publicist shook her head. "I have some of my people looking into it. For now we play it cool, offer your condolences."

"My, God. How could this happen?"

As it turned out, they didn't even continue the interview. He was ushered out in a hurry as the CNN producers reshuffled their lineup to focus on the breaking news.

Steiner was in complete shock. The loss of lives was awful, but his fifteen seconds seemed to be up. He sat in the dressing room watching the news streams. Pictures and video were coming in from foreign news services. So many bodies. Total destruction. His blood ran cold imagining what this could mean for his chances. Probably lost now. Swallowed by the horrific images being broadcast across oceans.

The dressing room slammed open and his publicist rushed into the room, her ever-present cell phone glued to her ear. "Right, thanks." She ended the call.

"Who was that?" Steiner asked.

"Do you trust me?" she asked, ignoring his question.

"I…uh…"

Her eyes bore into his. He wanted to back away, but he would have tipped his chair over.

"Do you trust me, Congressman?"

"Why? What's—"

She slapped him hard, his head turning to the side. He went to defend himself, but instead of repeating her assault, she said, "Listen. This is crunch time. I just got a bit of news that'll put you in primetime by this evening. It involves a lot of risk, but I think, if you listen to me, we can do it."

"What did you, I mean, what do we know?"

"It seems that the Marines were caught completely off guard. They didn't so much as defend themselves."

"But how is that possible considering—"

"Will you shut up and listen to me? This plays right into our hands. You've been saying that the Marine chain of command is ill-prepared to fight, taking unnecessary risks, leading young Americans to their death. This is the drum we need to beat right now. While the rest of America is mourning, we need to find the culprit. I've confirmed with two sources that this is legit."

"I don't know. This could really—"

"Yeah. You'll look like an asshole, like a thief desecrating the grave of American heroes. But don't you think their families deserve to know why they died? Don't you want to see those responsible brought to justice?"

Steiner never would have made that connection. Maybe she was right. After all, he'd already thrown in all his chips. Now that he thought about it, if they played their cards right, he could come out of this thing as a hero. The man who brought down the Marine Corps that led their Marines to slaughter. *Yes.*

He sat up straighter and shook off the stinging reminder of her slap.

"Okay. I'll do it."

Thirty minutes later, he'd returned to NPR. Same host, different topic. His publicist said the anchor had salivated over the story. They'd shored up the story on the way over, choosing to keep the details vague, citing anonymous sources and developing dialogues as excuses for not delving deeper.

By the time he returned to the same chair he'd sat in hours earlier, Congressman Tom Steiner was a changed man. Gone was the indecision. In its place was a man who'd found his mission, his ticket to stardom.

The cameraman gave them a thumbs up and the red light came on.

"Congressman Steiner, thank you for joining us again on such short notice."

"It's my pleasure."

"We don't have much time, so we'll cut right to the chase. Do you have information concerning the deadly attacks on Marine units where over three hundred casualties have already been confirmed?"

"I do, but let me first offer my sincere condolences to the families of the fallen."

The host nodded and bowed his head as if saying a silent prayer. After a quiet moment, his intense gaze returned to Steiner. "Congressman, what is the information you'd like to relay to the American people in the wake of this morning's attacks?"

Steiner closed his eyes and then opened them slowly. "It's my unfortunate duty to inform the American people that what I've warned about in prior testimony has come to pass."

"And what is that, Congressman?" The host leaned closer.

"The attacks, that could well be the deadliest single blow against combat troops since Vietnam, might have been prevented."

"Can you elaborate?"

They'd practiced the exchange before going on air. Steiner noticed how his host looked genuinely surprised despite already knowing what was coming. He'd have to talk to his new publicist about taking some acting classes if he was going to be on-air more often. It wouldn't do to look like an amateur.

"I can't go into specific details, considering the fluid situation on the ground, but I can say that the risks taken by Marine commanders, obsolete equipment in the hands of those poor enlisted Marines, and the complete disregard for the safety of their men by the chain of command led to these horrible atrocities."

Again the practiced shock on the face of the news anchor.

"But the Marines are the—"

"I know what you're going to say, Steve, but we were wrong. We've been given a crappy bill of goods. Those commanders were entrusted with the lives of their Marines and they failed." Steiner swiveled his chair and spoke directly to the camera, his finger pointing for effect. "For the lives of the American boys who died this morning, I will make it my personal mission to see that the entire Marine chain of command is prosecuted for its negligence, and that the Marine Corps be dismantled piece by piece."

CHAPTER 21

Glen Whitworth toasted himself for maybe the twentieth time. He'd been flipping from one TV channel to the next and three laptops lay arrayed across the dining room table, each streaming another feed.

The first couple hours were solemn affairs across mainstream media. And then Congressman Tom Steiner jumped off the top rope and slammed down with the game-changer. It sent shockwaves first across the Internet and then seeped into news crisis centers. Americans were calling for someone's head, but they didn't know whom. Terrorists? The White House? The Marine Corps?

Oh, the pundits blabbered back and forth. Some sided with Steiner while others staunchly defended Marine leadership. There had yet to be word from the White House or the Marine Commandant. Whitworth wished he could be a fly on the wall as the president and the top Marine general tried to get a grasp of the situation.

Fog of war ain't got shit on me! Whitworth wanted to scream to the world.

Unlike *Iron Man's* Tony Stark and his fictional post captivity epiphany, Whitworth knew his place in the world. He built killing machines and sold them to the highest bidder.

The Marine Corps had been a thorn in his company's side for years. He didn't know where or when it started, but since he could remember, his father had bristled at the stubborn Marine's consistent decision to avoid OrionTech's innovations. The latest, and possibly most costly, had been the F-35 program. Despite the deep Whitworth ties to the Army, Air Force and Navy, the Marine Commandant at the time had somehow swayed the rest. The program had gone to OrionTech's top competitor and had cost the Whitworth family untold billions.

Every time Glen Whitworth heard another report of misspending on the F-35 program, he wanted to gnash his teeth, imagining how he would've squeezed the government for every penny he could, without causing the rash of firestorms resulting from his competition's inability to control the situation. They were relative newcomers to the game, whereas the Whitworths had generations of experience dealing with the federal government. His grandfather used to tell young Glen stories when he'd had too much to drink. Glen's favorite was the one where his grandfather had, through a series of deliberate delays and supply fixing, sold the Army tens of thousands of mess kits, available at any surplus store for five dollars, at a whopping sum of twenty dollars a piece. He howled with glee every time he told that one.

The family skills had been passed down to Glen. He was a master at outmaneuvering his foe except when it came to the

Marines. Repeated attempts over the years had been met with icy glares and an escort to the door. Ah, but he had them on the ropes now. It was amazing what money could do. A well-placed bribe here and a little pressure exerted there. What was a few million when it meant billions, or even trillions in return?

Someone pounding at the front door shook him from his giggling. He was only wearing a pair of boxers, his growing belly hanging over like it was bragging, but he refused to put on any more clothes in his own posh suite. He padded to the door and looked through the peep hole. It was Gower.

Whitworth rolled his eyes, but opened the door.

"What have you done?" Gower hissed. His hair wasn't combed and he'd missed one of the buttons on his shirt. Whitworth could tell in a second that the man had been drinking.

"Come on in, Admiral. It looks like you could use a drink."

Gower stomped in behind him and Whitworth made himself a new drink. "Are you sure you won't have one?"

Gower looked like he was going to refuse, but gave Whitworth a quick nod.

Once Gower had taken a healthy swallow of his whiskey, the billionaire asked.

"So what's on your mind, Admiral?"

"You know goddamn well what's on my mind, Glen. Those Marines are dead. I've been trying to call you all morning. My phone hasn't stopped. They're putting everyone on lockdown."

"I don't see what this has to do with me," Whitworth said innocently, plucking a grape from the display on the table and popping it in his mouth.

"If I find out that you had anything to do with the murder of those Marines—"

Whitworth whirled around.

"You'll what? What will you do if I did?" He pressed his finger in Gower's chest, pushing him back a step. "I'll tell you what you're going to do if you know what's good for you. You are going to keep your mouth shut. You work for me remember?"

"I never signed up for—"

"You knew exactly what you signed up for, Joe. So now it's okay to have one of your best friends killed, but it's not okay to do it to a bunch of faceless Marines?"

Gower's eyes were wide with shock. Whitworth surmised that Gower had guessed about his involvement, but hadn't really believed it to be true. Well now he knew.

"But how...why did you think this was necessary? Why wasn't I told?" asked Gower, holding his drink with both hands as if it provided some necessary life force.

Whitworth swept his hand toward the laptops and their endless stream of video and data. "This is what I do. This is what the Whitworths have done for almost one hundred years. There are so many moving pieces that even if I tried to explain them all you wouldn't get past step three. Let's get one thing clear, right now. Knowing what you know now, you're either in or you're out. Make no mistake about what that means. You may be CEO of OrionTech, but I am the head. I make the decisions. I make the hard calls. Your job is to pick up the pieces and keep the machine running smoothly."

"And if I don't agree, what will you do, kill me?"

He'd said it in jest, but Whitworth's frown relayed the answer to the cocky admiral who had yet to realize his place. Gower's face went white, his hands shaking.

"Maybe you're right. Maybe you're not the right fit."

Whitworth grabbed the TV remote and changed the channel to a reggae music video channel and turned the volume up to its max. When he was halfway there another figure emerged from the door connecting Whitworth's unit to the adjoining luxury cottage. Gen. Duane Mason, Gower's old friend and roommate from the Naval Academy stepped in.

Admiral Gower's face scrunched in confusion, but then his body relaxed as Mason came closer.

"What are you doing here?" Gower asked over the thumping music.

"Same thing you are," said Mason, sipping from a bottle of Red Stripe beer.

"What?"

"I'm here for a job interview."

As Gower's eyes narrowed, Mason's right hand rose, a silenced pistol extended. The smooth trigger pull elicited the proper response, and the .22 caliber round spat out the end of the cylindrically extended barrel and entered Admiral Joseph Gower's head right between the eyes.

Gower's body flopped to the ground as Whitworth turned down the TV volume. Mason unscrewed the silencer and placed it and the pistol in his pocket.

"So? Do I have the job?"

Whitworth smiled at the man who'd not only manhandled nearly three companies of battle-hardened Marines, but had just shot his best friend, all in search of the mighty dollar, and a bit of power, of course. *This* was a man he could work with.

"You're hired."

CHAPTER 22

He'd been waiting for close to an hour. Not that he minded, but Headquarters Marine Corps was a zoo. Generals on down rushed to and fro while armed sentries guarded every door into the place. Cal sat in the hallway with Daniel Briggs and MSgt Willy Trent. Part of him felt like he was a lance corporal again, waiting to see the company gunny.

"Mr. Stokes," called a harried Marine major in desert cammies, his head poking out of one of the many doors.

"Right here," called Cal, rising with the others.

The major gave him a once over, obviously unsure of the man standing in front of him.

"I'm sorry, sir, I was told that it would only be you," said the major. Cal pegged him for an adjutant.

"They're with me," said Cal, motioning to his friends.

The major went to object, but a voice sounded from the office he stood protecting.

"Let them in, Major."

The major straightened up and waved them in.

The Commandant was talking to a group of generals and colonels. It reminded Cal of the time he'd been in the division CP before the invasion of Iraq. The Commandant's men all had the same looks. Hard. Focused. Rage simmering just under the surface, like fighters about to go into the boxing ring.

Gen. Winfield pointed to Cal and then his office. The Jefferson Group team headed that way, skirting around the huddle of men.

Two minutes later, the Commandant stepped in and closed the door behind him. His face deflated from the confident visage he'd shown moments earlier. Cal knew that look of loss, despair threatening to overcome the stubborn Marine's hard-charging persona.

"I'm sorry about Major Adams. He's taking his new gatekeeper role a little too seriously," said the Commandant, making a note on a pad on his desk.

"Not a problem, sir," said Cal.

"Have you heard the latest?"

"Only what we've seen on the news."

The Commandant shook his head. Pain in his eyes.

"Four hundred and ninety two dead," the Commandant muttered.

"And that's confirmed, sir?"

Winfield nodded. The number was twice what the media had initially reported.

"They want my head. Never could I have imagined something like this. Hitting us from the sidelines is one thing. But to kill our Marines—"

"With all due respect, sir," interrupted MSgt Trent, "those boys were murdered."

Again the pained nod from the Commandant.

They'd not only heard the updated reports of the rising death toll on their ride north, they'd also listened as a growing voice spread across the airwaves. There were calls for the Commandant to resign, for his general officer corps to be purged. If things could be worse, Cal couldn't imagine how. Winfield was right. Fighting a battle on Capitol Hill was one thing. Waking up to a slaughter was, well, unthinkable.

But Cal knew this wasn't the time to mourn. He'd lost men in the past and would probably lose more in the future. It was always the calm determination and support of men like Daniel Briggs, MSgt Trent and Gaucho that propelled him forward. He wondered if the new Commandant had anyone on his staff who had the balls to prod their boss. The top spot was a lonely post. Luckily for him, Cal wasn't about to keep his mouth shut.

Gen. Winfield's head rose and his hardened gaze met each Marine in turn.

"I want your honest opinion, gentlemen. As Marines. As men of honor. Could this have been prevented?"

Daniel spoke up first. "Sir, don't let the words of men like Congressman Steiner tarnish your faith in your men, your Marines. This was an act of unspeakable evil. Premeditated and probably planned down to the millisecond."

"He's right, sir," said Cal. "Those were Marine infantry companies, detachments expertly trained for their respective missions. They might not be as cowboy as the SEALs or as fancy as Delta, but there's no other unit I'd rather have at my back."

The Commandant digested their words, and then asked, "And do you think I should step down, resign my post?"

"Atten-hut!" barked MSgt Trent. All three Marines jumped to their feet and stood at precise positions of attention. "Sir, this Marine would like to respectfully say that your troops are with you. They believe in you. They know that you will do the right thing. The right thing is not giving the enemy what they want. The right thing is to come out swinging."

"But how do we do that when every unit we have is on lockdown and politicians and their constituents watch our every move? I'd like nothing more than to pick up a rifle and find whoever did this, but my hands are tied."

"Then let us do it, sir," said Cal. "Let us find them."

"But the risk…"

"Sir, with all due respect, we're Marines, too. The president has given the go-ahead and says that the final decision is yours. Let us do what we do best."

"And what's that, Mr. Stokes?" asked Winfield, life finally returning to his eyes, mingled with more than a hint of renewed interest.

"We find the bad guys and put them in the ground."

The Commandant's eyebrows rose. Cal had never told him the breadth of what they did for the president. All Winfield knew was that The Jefferson Group was some sort of problem solving asset in Zimmer's back pocket.

Gen. Winfield's eyes narrowed and the grim smile of a veteran commanding general appeared.

"Make it so."

———

Gaucho was waiting in the idling black SUV when the three Marines emerged from the headquarters building.

"How did it go?" asked Gaucho.

"He gave us the green light," said Cal.

C. G. COOPER

"So where do we start?"

Cal shrugged. "It's time for Neil, Jonas and Doc Higgins to earn their keep."

"Don't forget about Diane," said MSgt Trent.

Cal had almost forgotten about his girlfriend. She'd already reached out to her intelligence contacts, but they hadn't returned anything in the last two days. What they needed was a break. Other than Congressman Steiner, there were no other obvious targets. The surveillance they'd conducted on the New Jersey Democrat had turned up very little, nothing more than he was already saying on television. The only time he spent at his Alexandria apartment was to sleep. He never made any calls except to his new publicist and his staff. He was never contacted via email other than the rash of hate mail he'd received since announcing his intention to disband the Marine Corps.

Everything they'd seen seemed to indicate that Steiner had concocted and implemented the plan himself. There were still the 'anonymous' sources listed in his report to think about, but the increased focus on the congressman precluded The Jefferson Group from taking more overt action against Steiner. Besides, only in extreme cases would they kidnap and interrogate an elected official. Even though none of TJG's men liked it, so far it looked like Steiner was within his rights as an American. Free speech could be a double-edged sword, cutting into the very men and women who protected that most sacred American blessing even as it was exercised in supposed righteousness.

They had to be careful. But in the meantime, maybe something would go their way.

CHAPTER 23

Cassidy Ellwood was sick of watching the news. She'd had visitors at her home since returning from Orlando and it was all she could do to tolerate the presence of her well-meaning family. First the death of her husband, and now the senseless slaughter of his Marines.

Any bitterness she felt for the Marine establishment ended when it came to the troops. They had nothing to do with what her life had become. Most were innocent young men and women who had chosen to serve their country. She'd always found the presence of the younger enlisted refreshing. While other officers's wives avoided such interaction unless under obligation, Mrs. Ellwood loved her time with the junior enlisted and their families.

Her heart ached for their loss, for the pain now stabbing the hearts of their loved ones back home. She knew what Doug would do if he were alive: ask for a Marine division so he could find whoever was responsible and kill them.

Cassidy wouldn't have disagreed. She was just as much a Marine as her husband even though she'd never raised her right hand and said the oath. But she'd spent her life among them, caring for them, loving them.

As she wandered the small library that now served as her sanctuary (her family knew not to disturb her when she closed the doors), Cassidy Ellwood touched the countless books lining the shelves. They were all Doug's. She'd never realized how much he'd read, how hard he'd tried to be a good Marine officer. There was everything from U.S. Grant's autobiography to the writings of Sun Tzu. He even had books on the lives of Adolf Hitler and Che Guevara.

Doug had always said that in order to be an effective combat leader, he had to know the mind of the enemy. She was finally coming to grips with how much he'd studied his chosen field. Where she'd only experienced the time apart, the long hours at the office, Doug had been doing what he knew best, being a Marine.

Cassidy had to admit, he was a damn good Marine. There'd been a lot of talk about him becoming Commandant one day. While she knew what that meant, she'd been too consumed with maintaining appearances and trying to keep her sons and their families close to enjoy the prospect. Truth be told, she secretly would have hated him for taking the top post. There'd been too much buried for so long.

The trip to Orlando was supposed to be the fix. It sure had felt like it. They'd become friends again, lovers even. She felt the passion she'd first encountered when the athletic 2nd Lt Doug Ellwood marched into her life. She cried as she remembered his embrace, his sweet words, his smile. The smell in the library reminded her of him, like old leather, military canvas bags and pencil shavings. She missed him, wanted to hold him and never let go.

As her hand grazed over the middle row of books, her finger slipped over a red tassel. She stopped. It was a bookmark. Now she remembered that she'd given it to Doug years before, on one of their many moves cross-country. She pulled the book out. It was an old planner, the corners bent and the cover faded.

It had the emblem of the United States Naval Academy in the center with the year 1975 in calligraphy underneath. It was from Doug's first year at the Academy.

She flipped it open to the first page that had his unmistakable chicken scratch handwriting.

Sworn in today. Got thrashed. Pretty good food at the chow hall.

Cassidy smiled. That sounded like Doug as an eighteen year old Plebe. He loved to eat and had somehow maintained his weight despite his proclivity for huge meals.

She flipped to another page.

Football practice was tough (two guys puked) but a lot easier than class. I'm not sure I'm going to get through English.

Cassidy knew that it had taken Doug some time to warm up to academics. He'd told her that his high school had only cared about what he did on the football field and covered for him with his grades. He'd essentially gone to the Academy with a middle school education.

She turned the page to where the bookmark was waiting. It was a laminated picture of the California coast somewhere north of Camp Pendleton. She set it aside, and read that day's entry.

Coach made me go to a tutor. His name is Gower.
I could tell he didn't like me, but he knows his stuff.
Hopefully this helps.

Cassidy knew Joe Gower well and was surprised that she didn't know the story of how he and Doug had met. They always said they'd become friends at the Academy, like that was explanation enough. Even more curious was the fact that Doug had circled the name *Gower* with a red pen.

She flipped to the next page and it was the same thing. A couple more pages forward and he'd written,

Joe Gower introduced me to his roommate D. Mason.
Seems like a knucklehead, but a nice enough guy.
Going to take them with me on libo this weekend.

This time both Gower and Mason were circled in red. Cassidy Ellwood quickly scanned through the rest of the calendar diary. Every mention of Gower or Mason elicited a red circle around their names. Her breath caught as she turned to the last page.

They made me do it. I love you. - Doug

Cassidy's stomach clenched. Did this mean what she thought? Who should she call? What should she do?

Then the memory from Orlando came to her. Those Marines who'd come for Scotty Winfield. *Stokes.*

He'd given her broken heart a glimmer of hope when he'd said that maybe there'd been a reason for Doug's death. That conversation replayed in her head as she pulled out her cell phone and looked for his number. There it was.

She clicked on the number and the phone began to ring. Her heart was racing, mind flailing as it tried to comprehend.

"Stokes," came the answer.

"Mr. Stokes, this is Cassidy Ellwood."

"Yes, Ma'am. I'm sorry I haven't kept in touch, but things—"

"I've found something you should see."

There was a pause on the other end.

"Is there any way this could wait until—"

"No. You have to come now."

"Yes, Ma'am. Can I get your address?"

She gave it to him.

"You're in luck. We're right down the road in Arlington. Can we stop by in ten minutes?"

"The sooner the better."

"Okay. We'll see you soon, Mrs. Ellwood."

Cassidy Ellwood placed the phone on Doug's desk and hugged the old diary to her chest. Maybe she would finally have her answer.

CHAPTER 24

WASHINGTON, D.C.

3:16PM, DECEMBER 9TH

Congressman Tony McKnight flipped from one social media account to the next as he perused the day's news. Not only had his office phone been ringing off the hook, his constituents were clogging every online profile he had. Conservatives smelled blood and they wanted it yesterday.

There was talk of a march being planned for the following weekend to rally support for the beleaguered Marines. Marine recruiters were turning away prospects in droves, but the biggest uproar came from Marines who'd left active duty. There were pictures of long lines of young and old wanting back in to avenge the deaths of their brothers.

Tom Steiner had been on every major news network, calling for the ouster of General Winfield and his cohorts. McKnight would have chuckled if he hadn't been walking into another emergency session with President Zimmer. The Florida Republican had been one of the first politicians called in after news of the attacks surfaced. McKnight had a front row seat among the president's crisis response team.

He wondered what they'd think if they knew he was behind it all. Rep. Steiner crowed from the rooftops because of the study Tony McKnight had funded. It was easy to keep his name out of it. Hell, the Navy and Army had done most of the work for him. Despite what they were saying on television, there were plenty of officers in both services who would secretly celebrate the Marine Corps's undoing. They'd been trying to do it for over a century, and now might just be the time. McKnight knew they were waiting to see how the political tussle would pan out.

Then there was the money behind the entire operation, willingly supplied by Glen Whitworth. The smug military supplier didn't know of McKnight's involvement either. They were acquainted, and had mingled at fundraisers and junkets, but McKnight knew much more about Whitworth's ambition than the billionaire knew about him. Thanks to a tipsy conversation they'd shared two years before, McKnight understood the rich man's hatred of the Corps. He'd merely planted the seed through others and watched it grow. Intermediaries, minor politicians yearning for power, and military officers looking for advancement were easy to manipulate. They'd done the heavy lifting. Once the greased machine started moving, there was no stopping it.

So while he listened and nodded as Gen. McMillan briefed the president on the latest efforts to retrieve the Marine dead, McKnight marveled at the breadth of his scheme. Maybe he'd have to write a book some day. He could call it *How to Get Anything You Want on Capitol Hill*, or maybe *Tony McKnight: Master of Manipulation*. Nah. Better to keep it to himself. After all, how many clever politicians could Washington hold?

Cal, Daniel, Gaucho and MSgt Trent climbed in the car. No one said a word as Gaucho backed out of the driveway and headed back to their hotel. Cal had Gen. Ellwood's diary in his lap. Mrs. Ellwood had told them the story of how she'd found her husband's journal and who the two men were whose names had been circled time after time.

"Joe Gower is a two star in the Navy. Submariner and an academic. Cerebral. Last we heard from him he was at the Pentagon on his twilight tour. The same for Duane Mason. He's a major general in the Army, came up through Special Forces. Again, I'm not exactly sure what he does now, but Duane always pushed my patience."

"How so?" Cal had asked.

"Duane has always had a wandering eye. His ex-wife and I were friends for a time. You wouldn't believe the stories. I didn't at the time, but as he moved up the ranks his demeanor changed. He was more dirty old man than casual flirt."

She'd made Cal promise to stay in touch and keep her apprised of the situation.

"Hey, boss, that name Mason rang a bell," said Gaucho, not taking his eyes off the road as he pulled into traffic.

"Yeah?"

"There was a Colonel Mason when I was with Delta. Never served under him, but I thought you should know."

"Could you reach out to some of your old friends and see what they know?"

"No problem."

A Marine general, a Navy admiral and an Army general. Cal wondered how it had all started. He'd thought about staying at the Ellwood's to search the place for more clues, but they just didn't have the time or the manpower. The thought gave him an idea. Maybe it was time to enlist some more help.

He pulled out his phone and tapped on Special Agent Robbie Barrett's phone number.

"Special Agent Barrett."

"Barrett, it's Cal Stokes."

"Oh. Hey."

"Look, something's come up. I was wondering if you had anyone to spare."

"Are you kidding? We're sending every agent we can overseas to investigate the Marine thing."

Cal should've known. Maybe he could throw Barrett a bone.

"What if I told you that this might have something to do with that?"

Barrett was silent for a long moment, and then answered, "You have my attention."

"We just found something that could connect General Ellwood's death to the attacks."

It wasn't the whole truth, but Barrett didn't need to know that.

"Okay. What do you need from me?"

"Could you have someone in the D.C. area do a thorough search of the Ellwood residence?"

"Sure."

The answer came too quick.

"Really?"

"Yeah. I'm in Alexandria."

That surprised Cal.

"What are you doing up here?"

"I can't tell you that."

Cagey bastard, thought Cal.

"Do you have anyone with you?"

"I've got another agent."

"Okay. How quickly can you get there?"

"I can finish what I'm doing and be there in about an hour."

"I'll let Mrs. Ellwood know. Here's the address." Cal rattled it off and thanked Barrett for the help. He figured it was only a matter of time before the NCIS knew the whole story. Might as well use some of their expertise to unravel the mystery. Barrett was probably salivating at the chance to be the hero.

"You sure that was a good idea?" asked MSgt Trent from the front passenger seat.

"Not really, but it'll free us up to find out about Gower and Mason."

Trent nodded but didn't look convinced.

Gaucho honked the horn as a Toyota Tacoma cut them off turning through a congested intersection. Cal went to say something when the front windshield splintered and Gaucho grunted. His foot must have been on the pedal because as he slumped forward, they shot into the intersection, swerving wildly and heading into the wrong lane. Barreling toward them was a semi, its horn already blaring.

CHAPTER 25

His timing was perfect. The shot dead on.

The sniper watched the scene unfold through his scope, time slowing as the SUV careened toward the semi. *This is more like it*, he thought, congratulating himself on a successful stalk. His employer would be happy.

He was about to crawl back out of his position, happy that his task was nearly complete. It wasn't necessary that Cal Stokes and his men die. If they did, so much the better. No, his boss had been clear. "Put them out of commission," he'd said.

A head-on collision with a semi would do just that. He smiled.

But fate was a funny thing. Miraculously, as the very last nano second, the SUV veered out of the way and plowed through two cars and thumped over a curb into the green space bordering an apartment complex.

The sniper's finger settled on the trigger, anxious to take another shot, but it never came. Stokes's SUV plunged out of sight.

They'd paid a lot of cash to that truck driver, an ex-con who was happy to take the money in exchange for his role in the "accident." Now the sniper had another loose end to tie up.

He slid the view hole in the back of the dated Pontiac closed and backed into the second row.

"Where to?" asked the driver, a man sent by his employer to help the sniper in any way needed. He didn't mention the shot or whether the sniper had made the hit. He knew his place.

"Drop me off at the hotel," ordered the sniper as he stowed his rifle in its carrying case.

Two times he'd missed his mark. The last time that had happened he'd nearly been blown to bits by a Taliban RPG. It still brought back nightmares on occasion. He shook the thought away and focused on how to best tell his boss that he'd missed again.

They'd finally come to a stop against a green dumpster. Cal and Daniel had braced themselves in the back as MSgt Trent had somehow held Gaucho's limp body back off the steering wheel and managed to divert the vehicle's trajectory.

The airbags had deployed and were now losing their pressure. Everyone was moving except for Gaucho. By the time Cal had unfastened his seatbelt, Trent was checking his best friend for signs of life.

"I don't see any blood," said Trent, ripping Gaucho's T-shirt open. By then Daniel and Cal were outside the vehicle scanning for threats.

Cal popped the driver's side door open.

"He's breathing," announced Trent, his relief evident. "Lucky Mexican was wearing his level four."

"Get off me you big ape," moaned Gaucho, his face a mask of pain.

"You okay?" asked Trent.

"I'll live."

Cal shook his head. Too close.

"Let's get him to the hospital."

"I'm okay, boss. Just need to lie down for a second," said Gaucho with a grimace. "I think I got lucky. It grazed me." He pointed to the open door and a ragged hole in the leather arm rest.

"You think we can drive this thing out of here?" Trent asked Cal.

Cal gave the SUV a once over. It had seen better days, but other than a hole in the windshield, the deployed airbags and the crushed collision points around the front bumper, it looked intact.

"Help Gaucho out and I'll see if it starts."

Waving off the help, Gaucho eased himself out of the vehicle and leaned on one arm against the hood. Cal slid in and tried the ignition. It started up with barely a stutter.

After cutting away the airbags, everyone piled in just as curious tenants started coming out of their apartments. It was only a matter of time before someone called the cops, a complication Cal didn't need.

Keeping as low a profile as they could inside the vehicle, they left the apartment complex through a narrow service entrance, Daniel watching for tails as Cal and Trent scanned for threats up ahead. Within minutes they were back on Leesburg Pike, headed to Arlington.

The sniper hung up the phone and slammed his palm on the back of the headrest. It had been a one-way conversation. The last thing his boss had said before ending the call was, "You've got one more strike."

He knew his personal attachment to his employer only went so far. When it came to business, his boss didn't care. The sniper glanced at the driver and wondered if that's why the man had been sent, to look after him, maybe even to take him out should the need arise. He would've done the same thing.

The sniper slid his pistol out of his pocket and held it on his lap. He'd just have to keep an eye on the guy until he got dropped off. He had one shot left. Best not to test his employer's limits again.

HEADQUARTERS MARINE CORPS

As Cal pulled into the only spot they could find, blocks from the busy headquarters building, Gaucho pulled his ringing cell phone out of a pocket with a wince. Cal was surprised when his team leader answered the call instead of ignoring it.

"Yeah?"

Cal watched Gaucho's eyebrows rise in the rearview mirror. Gaucho motioned for the others' attention.

"Hey, you mind if I put you on speaker?"

The answer must have been yes because a moment later Gaucho held up the phone so everyone could hear.

"You still there?" came the gravelly voice.

"Yeah. Hey, say again what you just told me."

"You sure you're secure?"

"Yeah, go ahead."

"Okay, like I was saying, I just caught wind of some squirrely shit going on. You told me to call if I heard anything, so I did."

"What did you hear?"

"I overheard one of my new guys, a real piece of shit if you ask me, don't know how he hasn't been in the clink yet, starts blabbin' about getting out and landing a new job. I didn't think it was anything until he gets kinda quiet and in a roundabout way ties it to what's all over the news."

"How?"

"I can't remember exactly what he said, but it was something about his friend taking care of those fucking jarheads real good. He laughed it off and said it was a joke, but this guy, I don't know man. The way he is—"

"Hey, man, can I put you on hold?"

"Sure."

Gaucho's muted the conversation and looked at Cal. "What do you think?"

"Who's that you're talking to?"

"Old Delta buddy, senior man at one of the Bragg squadrons. I called him a couple days ago, told him to keep an eye out. He's on my short list to bring to TJG if he ever retires."

It could've been an idiot running off at the mouth. Cal had heard his fair share of dirtbags brag about things they knew nothing about, but until they found out more about Gower and Mason, there were few leads to follow.

"Do you think he can keep the guy confined to quarters until we get there?"

"Sure."

Gaucho took the phone off mute and relayed the request to his comrade.

"No problem. I can keep him there for twenty-four hours without raising any cain. How quick can you get here?"

"We'll be there tonight," said Gaucho.

"All right. See you soon."

CHAPTER 26

Congressman Tom Steiner sat across the small table and did his best to keep still. He'd found over the preceding days (or rather his publicist had pointed it out) that he liked to fidget when he got excited. Rather than look animated, his handler said it made him look spastic.

Steiner didn't see it that way, but he vowed to keep her happy. That included clasping his hands either on his lap when sitting on a couch or on a flat surface when the setting permitted.

"Congressman, you've caused quite a stir with your accusations following the deadly attack on Marine units deployed overseas. Why do you think it's important to have this conversation now and not after the families of the dead are allowed to grieve?"

It was the same tired question that reporters were trying to cram down his throat.

"Like I've said before, now is the time because the pain is fresh in our minds. Did we wait months or years after 9/11 to retaliate? No. I can't begin to understand the grief of those poor families, but I can do something about it."

The news anchor's face was just short of a sneer.

"And you think that going after the Marine chain of command is what we should do? Why not go after the enemy who killed the Marines? Shouldn't *that* be what we focus on?"

Steiner gave his best patient smile.

"I'm not privy to those conversations, but I'm sure the rest of the military has things well in hand. But this is more than just about good versus evil. What we've uncovered is a fouled system whose negligence cost America the lives of hundreds of its brave men in uniform. Yes, we will find the culprits behind these attacks, but we will also bring down the hierarchy that allowed it to happen."

The rest of the interview was tense, the conservative host doing his best to get under Steiner's skin, but the New Jersey congressman felt that he'd handled it well.

"How did I do?" Steiner asked his publicist after it was over. She was scrolling through her ever-present phone.

"You could have been a little more authoritative without looking patronizing, but you keep getting better."

Steiner knew that was the closest to a compliment he was going to get. At least they'd gotten past the point of a thirty minute nitpick after every interview.

"Where to next?" he asked, wondering if there was time to grab a quick bite to eat. He was starving.

"You're finished for the day," she said without looking up. "Bright and early tomorrow."

She left without saying another word, her phone already back at her ear as she railed against someone else. Steiner shook his head and grinned. She was expensive, and a real hard-ass, but damn was she good. His star was rising fast despite the controversial nature of his platform. He wondered where it might take him. The senate, maybe, or even the governor's mansion?

Rep. Steiner shrugged on his coat and went to find his driver.

Just as he was getting into the Lincoln Towncar, someone called his name.

He turned to see four men in dark suits approaching. For a moment his stomach twisted.

"Sir, United States Secret Service."

"How may I be of assistance, gentlemen?" Steiner tried to sound confident, but he couldn't help but feel nervous.

"Sir, the president would like a word."

Steiner almost told the man that he had somewhere to be, but thought better of it. He was curious.

"Should we follow you or…"

"It would save time if you came in our vehicle, sir."

Steiner nodded and followed the four agents to their armored SUV.

Twenty minutes later, Congressman Steiner stepped into the Oval Office. There was a fire crackling in the hearth, but no one was there.

"The president is on his way, sir," said the Secret Service agent who motioned to the couches and then departed.

Steiner told himself not to be in awe of the place, but he couldn't help looking around the room. Never in his years in the House had he been invited to the symbolic center of the nation's power. The fact that he was there now added to his estimation that his clout was growing.

President Zimmer walked in a minute later followed by his chief of staff, Travis Haden, and Steiner's fellow New Jersey Democrat, Ezra Matisse. He couldn't read their faces. It didn't help that no one offered to shake his hand when he stood.

"Thanks for coming, Tom," said the president.

"It is my pleasure, Mr. President. How may I be of service?"

"I'll cut right to the chase. This thing with the Marine Corps has got to stop. Can't you see the damage you're doing?"

So that was why he'd been summoned. Steiner could've laughed.

"I'm not sure I see it that way, Mr. President."

Zimmer's eyes went cold. "I asked Ezra to join us as a witness. You two go back a long time, and I figured that if I couldn't convince you maybe he could."

"Convince me of what?" Steiner asked innocently. He was enjoying this immensely.

"Drop the proposal."

So there it was. The president was trying to keep him in his place. Steiner wasn't about to let that happen. He didn't want to go back to being on the fringe.

"I believe it is well within my right to examine any entity under our government's purview. That is especially the case when there is a preponderance of evidence to suggest fraud, waste and outright negligence."

"You don't honestly believe that load of crap, do you, Tom?"

"Yes I do."

Zimmer shook his head.

"And there's nothing I can do to change your mind?"

Steiner sat up a little straighter. "I don't think there is."

"And what if I gave you one chance to drop it, or face the consequences?"

"If you're trying to threaten me, Mr. President…"

"Oh you'll know when I'm threatening you, Tom. What I'm doing now is giving you a warning. There are things going on that apparently you have no idea about."

"And what would those things be?"

Steiner had everything he needed. He'd weighed the risks and found that he liked the idea of being the whistleblower. It only added to his growing fame.

"I'm not going to tell you. You'll just have to trust me. But I will promise you that if you drop your accusation right now, things will go back to the way they were. No hard feelings."

Steiner's eyes narrowed. The president was trying to manipulate him. Where was the young Massachusetts congressman who'd bravely waved the liberal agenda? The man now residing in the Oval Office had obviously been poisoned by the likes of Travis Haden and that Marine general McMillan. Zimmer had chosen to put the blinders on.

"Mr. President, the investigation into the Marine Corps's wrongdoing and the legislation that will see them wiped off our budget will come to pass. I will not be dissuaded. I stand by my sources and the information they had provided. Open your eyes, Mr. President. The Marines are playing the same game they've been playing for years. They brag about being the tip of the spear when, in fact, their leadership ability has gone the same way as their obsolete equipment. I will not stand by as more Americans are pumped through their corrupt and antiquated pipeline. That is a promise."

Steiner expected the president to deny the charges, scream, shake his fist, anything. But instead Zimmer looked to Rep. Matisse, who shook his head sadly. Zimmer nodded then looked back to Steiner.

"Very well. Here's what's going to happen. As soon as you step out of this office, you will be escorted to the Hoover Building where you will be questioned by the director of the FBI himself."

Steiner felt his face color. "I don't see why—"

"I'm not finished," snapped Zimmer. "You had your chance. Now, as I was saying, you will be questioned by the director and his team of expert interrogators. This isn't your witch hunt anymore, Congressman. This is a matter of national security. If they—"

Steiner wanted to roll his eyes. National security. It had become the excuse for the government to arrest and question anyone. What was next, a new Gestapo?

"This is completely illegal," said Steiner, confident that his trip to FBI headquarters would be brief. Now that he thought about it, the highly criminal act could be used to his benefit. The media would love to hear how the president had not only threatened him, but enlisted the FBI by using questionable tactics. Maybe the next target on Steiner's list should be the FBI. That could be his new image. Tom Steiner, rooting out corruption at its core. "This conversation is over." Steiner went to stand.

"Travis, what do you think would happen if I stepped over there and decked Mr. Steiner?"

Steiner stopped moving.

"I wouldn't recommend it, Mr. President," answered Haden. "Have you ever hit someone in the face?"

Zimmer shook his head.

"Hurts more than you think. Now the gut or the solar plexus are much easier on the knuckles. I wouldn't want you spraining your wrist before your meeting with the Israelis in the morning."

Steiner couldn't believe what he was hearing. The two men looked like they were having an idle conversation in the men's locker room.

"I don't have to stand here and listen to this," said Steiner, grabbing his coat from the arm of the sofa.

"You're right, Tom. But let me tell you something before you go. You may think that my line about this being a threat to our national security is totally bogus, but you'd be wrong. Now, I'm not sure where you're getting your information, and I have a feeling that you don't know either. Frankly, I've never been too impressed with your street smarts. Have you stopped to consider that whomever gave you the information might be involved in the attacks on our Marines? Did that possibility ever enter your brain?"

The president laughed. "I can see by the look on your face that you didn't." He turned to Rep. Matisse. "Well, you were right, Ezra. I should've just handed this to the FBI."

"You were trying to be fair, Mr. President," said Matisse, casting Steiner a disgusted look.

"I guess we're past that now." Zimmer sighed. "Have a nice trip, Tom. I don't think we'll be seeing each other again."

Taking his cue to leave, Steiner strode to the door and hesitated as his hand closed around the handle. For the first time since the Marine escapade had started, he wondered if it had been a wise choice to step onto his current path. When he opened the door, his anxiety only grew. Waiting for him were the director of the FBI and a handful of agents. The director spoke before Steiner could unhinge his locked jaw.

"Good evening, Congressman. I'm so looking forward to speaking with you."

CHAPTER 27

The Gulfstream G650ER with the tail marking TJG911 taxied across the runway to where a World War II-era jeep waited alongside a large white passenger van.

Since the area was on Gaucho's home turf (the home of 1st Special Forces Operation Detachment-Delta [aka Delta Force] being next door at Ft. Bragg), he exited The Jefferson Group's private plane first, followed by MSgt Trent, Cal, Daniel and Dr. Higgins.

There was a scruffy looking middle-aged man sitting on the hood of the jeep, smoking a cigarette. The guy didn't look like a Delta veteran to Cal, but the Marine knew that meant little. Delta boys were known for being invisible. This guy looked like he'd just closed up his pub before coming to meet them. The man hopped off the olive drab relic.

"You're still as ugly as ever," the man said to Gaucho.

"And you're still older than my abuelito."

Both men grinned. Their resulting handshake turned into a hug.

Gaucho presented his old friend to the others.

"Gentlemen, this is Karl. He and I go back a long ways."

Cal guessed that Karl was either a command sergeant major or very close to it. Whereas active duty Marines might cringe at introducing themselves without mentioning rank, he knew the other services held no such scruples. It was just another difference in the culture, but for the guys in Delta Force it went much deeper. Anonymity was one of their best assets.

Karl chuckled and appraised the visitors as he took one last inhale from his cigarette and flicked it away. "Let me guess, you boys are Marines. I can always tell by your perfect posture." He shook Cal's hand.

It was Cal's turn to laugh. "And I thought they only let ex-cons with mommy complexes join Delta."

Karl raised an eyebrow and glanced at Gaucho, who just shrugged as if to say, "I told you so."

"Looks like you've found another family of smart asses, my friend," Karl said to Gaucho. "Anyway, welcome to North Carolina. If you wouldn't mind stepping over to the waiting van, we'll head straight to our next appointment."

Fifteen minutes later, the vehicles pulled off the road and onto a dirt trail wide enough to accommodate a tank. It reminded Cal of his time in that other North Carolina military retreat, Camp Lejeune. He couldn't see the tall pine trees bordering the lane, but Cal knew they were there.

Once the drivers had put their vehicles in park, the men stepped out into the brisk December air. They'd parked just outside what looked to be a bunker, complete with an illuminated mailbox on which someone had written *HOME* in flowing white lettering.

They followed Karl into the bunker where two men, both sporting matching beards and Arabic robes, sat playing cards.

"Whatcha say, Karl?" one of the men asked. Cal noticed the automatic weapons propped against each man's leg, and a pistol each on the card table.

"The asshole give you any problems?" asked Karl.

"He wouldn't shut up for a while, but he finally got the point."

Cal wondered if the point had been a kick or a punch.

Karl led the way down a dimly lit concrete corridor. It looked like some ammo dumps Cal had visited as a kid. They'd mostly been filled in or shut off over the years.

They came to a door that looked like it belonged in a horror movie instead of on a military installation. It even had spiked iron bars that served to keep hands from sticking through the small window.

Karl slid the rusted latch aside and pulled open the door. A flick of a switch later and the small sandbagged room was bathed in fluorescent light. There was a man on the floor, mouth duct taped closed, and his arms and legs hog-tied with parachord.

"Well, Bobby, I brought you some new friends," said Karl, stepping over and ripping the duct tape off the man's mouth, taking a fair chunk of his growing mustache with it.

"You, motherfucker! Wait until I get out of here, I'm gonna—"

The rest of the sentence disappeared along with the air in Bobby's lungs resulting from the kick from Karl's boot.

"Listen up, shit head. If you know what's good for you, tell them everything you know."

"Fuck you," Bobby managed to wheeze out. This guy was probably what the world thought a Delta operator should look like. Tall, muscular and accustomed to pain. He even had the look that made recruiting posters.

As Karl went to kick the man again, Cal stopped him with an outstretched arm.

"You mind if we have a go?" he asked.

"You talking about working him over, because I hope you know what you're doing," said Karl, taking a step to the side.

"It just so happens that my friend back there," Cal pointed to Dr. Higgins, "is a master at getting guys like this to talk."

Karl looked at Higgins and then back to Cal. Cal knew what he was thinking. The guy on the ground was undoubtedly trained to evade questioning for as long as he could. Karl was probably thinking that the chubby guy with glasses was the last guy to make Bobby talk. With an amused shrug, Karl said, "Be my guest."

Dr. Higgins stepped into the room with his well-worn leather doctor's bag. "Do you have a place we can lie him flat on his back, on a gurney perhaps?" asked Higgins, who was completely at ease despite being the only non-warrior in the group.

"I'm sure we can rig something up."

Not long after, Cal's team had managed to strap Bobby by his wrists and ankles with a set of orange truck cables provided by Karl. He was laying on top of a pile of plywood the size of a door and stacked waist high.

It took their collective strength, and a heavy dose of a MSgt Trent headlock, to get the man secured. Once they did, he knew he wasn't going anywhere.

Dr. Higgins was lining up his tools on the card table provided by the two guards who were now watching the show with unabashed curiosity.

"Okay, gentlemen, may I get started?" asked Dr. Higgins, rubbing his latex gloved hands together.

Cal nodded and Higgins approached his subject.

"Now, before we begin, what may I call you," Higgins asked the man.

"Fuck you," Bobby spat.

"I'm not sure I can call you that. How about Robert? That is your given name?"

Bobby nodded with more than a little reluctance.

"Very well, Robert, what I am about to administer will not be painful. In fact, what my subjects have told me is that the less you struggle, the easier it is."

Higgins showed Bobby the two syringes in his hand. The motion produced a new round of writhing, which elicited a sharp elbow jab in Bobby's abdomen from MSgt Trent. Bobby's struggle stopped as he gasped for air.

"As I said, this won't hurt…"

"What the hell is going on here?" came a booming voice from just outside the room. A slightly older and heavier version of Gaucho stomped into the room. The man had a shaggy white beard and his blazing eyes zeroed in on Karl, then down to Bobby, and back to Karl.

"I was going to tell you…" started Karl.

"And who are these guys?" the man asked, pointing to Cal and his team.

"Maybe we should step outside for a minute, Colonel," suggested Karl.

He got a curt nod in response as "The Colonel" marched back out of the room. "That fucking needle better not touch Bobby," he said over his shoulder.

Karl, Cal and Gaucho followed the incensed leader back out into the cold.

"Sir, I can explain," said Karl.

"Let's not start with the *sir* crap, Karl. Now tell me what the hell is going on."

Karl nodded. "Vince, this is my old friend Gaucho and this over here is Cal."

"I know you, don't I?" Vince said, pointing at Gaucho.

Gaucho smiled.

"Philippines, right?"

Gaucho nodded. Some of the steam seemed to release from the colonel's attitude.

"And who's this kid?" he asked, motioning to Cal.

"Cal Stokes, Colonel." Cal extended his hand. The Army colonel looked at it for a moment and then shook it.

"Something tells me that you're the ringleader of this little party, Mr. Stokes. How about you tell me what the fuck is going on before I have you escorted to the stockade."

Cal nodded and began the story.

Vince listened as Cal told him about the possible connection between the man tied up a few feet away and the death of hundreds of United States Marines. He even went so far as to tell the colonel that The Jefferson Group worked directly for the president. Unlike how most people would've reacted, Vince's demeanor didn't change at the mention of the

Commander in Chief. Cal knew that was because more so than even the recently flashy Navy SEALs, Delta was involved in more black sanctioned covert ops than any other force in the military arsenal. These guys were handpicked not only for their talents, but for the fact they knew how to keep their mouths shut and stay under the radar.

"So you think that the guy in glasses back there can make one of *my* guys talk in less than an hour?" Vince asked, the look on his face more amused than incredulous.

"I know he can," said Cal.

"And you really think that former Delta guys were involved in the death of your Marines?"

Cal didn't want to point fingers. He knew what it felt like to hear that some idiot Marine had gone and killed his wife or committed some other horrid act. Placing blame on men who at one time could've been under Vince's command would be inappropriate until they had solid proof.

"We don't know that yet," Cal answered truthfully. "All we know is what Karl overheard. If the guy's full of shit, we'll be out of your hair before midnight."

Vince thought it over. "And you're willing to stick your neck out for this, Karl?"

"I am," Karl answered without hesitating.

Vince grunted. "Okay then. Let's go see what this doctor can do."

"I think you'll be amazed," said Cal, remembering the first time he'd seen Higgins at work. The former CIA interrogator was part artist and part mad scientist.

Vince snorted. "We'll see." He headed back towards the bunker entrance then turned suddenly. "I need you to promise me something, Mr. Stokes."

"If I can."

"If this turns out to be true, if former Delta were involved, or even former soldiers, I want you to do everything you can to convince the president that we want in. I'll help you take those assholes down."

Cal grinned. "I don't think that'll be a problem, Vince."

CHAPTER 28

Congressman McKnight sipped his piping hot coffee and settled in for what he privately called "The Steiner Show." Every day he either watched a live or recorded version of Rep. Tom Steiner's latest interview. It was sort of a guilty pleasure for the Floridian, watching the New Jersey native spout the very twisted truth that McKnight had concocted. There were even specific lines that he'd penned himself that Steiner had repeated verbatim.

It was too good not to watch. Steiner had been ripe for it. Struggling to make a name even after multiple terms in the House, the poor guy was practically begging for a shot at the big leagues.

Now he had it, and McKnight had to admit, after a couple minor stumbles, the guy was catching on. He'd perfected his message. It didn't hurt that the media newbie had a powerhouse publicist in his corner, yet another masterful introduction made by McKnight, in a roundabout way, of course. She'd ensured that the congressman never went into a battle he couldn't win, or at least fight to a stalemate. For the most part that meant taking the interviews with left-leaning news outlets, and also avoiding round table discussions where Steiner might get pushed into a corner. The debates would come soon, but for now it was fine that Steiner was singing from his soapbox.

So as the news anchor began his daily monologue, McKnight was looking forward to the show. He wondered if his latest piece of intel had filtered into Steiner's hands yet.

"Our first guest of the day, Congressman Thomas Steiner, will be unable to join us this morning. In his place we will be talking to a panel of experts who…"

McKnight set his coffee mug down and stared at the television screen, his morning unsettled for the time being. He was tempted to call Steiner's publicist and find out what was going on, but he held his hand. If she put two and two together, that could link McKnight to Steiner. That was something he couldn't afford to have happen.

Instead of worrying about it, he muted the television and diverted his attention to his ever-filling email inbox.

Eleven messages in, his direct line rang. That could only mean one thing.

"Congressman McKnight."

"Good morning, Tony."

"Good morning, Mr. President."

"I'm late for a breakfast meeting, but I wanted to give you an update on our situation."

Ask and you shall receive, thought McKnight.

"I'm all ears."

"Tom Steiner won't be a problem anymore."

McKnight's voice almost caught in his throat.

"Oh?"

"I can't give you the details until we know more, but suffice it to say that we've linked him to some of the sources in his report."

McKnight wanted to scream.

"Wow. That's good news. How did it happen?" he somehow managed to ask.

The president chuckled, the sound serving to further rattle McKnight's nerves. "I've got a couple tricks up my sleeve."

"Any that you could share?"

"Let's just say that I know some people who are very good at what they do."

"That's good to hear, Mr. President. Does that mean that the investigation into the Marine deaths is heating up?" *Please say no.*

"I can't get into that over the phone. Maybe you can stop by later and I'll fill you in. You have been in on this from the beginning, and I'll say again how much I appreciate your help."

McKnight saw the silver lining, grabbed it, and tried his best to push his anxiety away.

"It's been my pleasure. What time would you like me to stop by?"

"I'm meeting with Travis and General McMillan after lunch, I think it's one o'clock. Stop by then?"

"I'm putting it in my calendar now."

"Great. See you soon."

The line went dead, but McKnight kept the phone to his ear, gripping it until he felt the plastic start to give. He somehow resisted the urge to slam the receiver down, settling it back in its place.

Think.

How much did the president know? McKnight wondered if Steiner was in custody or merely in self-imposed exile. He guessed the former, considering the president's confident tone. McKnight wasn't concerned with being caught. There was nothing to connect him to the report or Steiner. But if the president's people found out about the other part of McKnight's scheme, the part involving OrionTech, Gower and Mason, things could go the wrong way quickly.

No plan was ever one hundred percent foolproof, but McKnight prided himself with his cunning and planning. He'd walked through every outcome he could think of. He'd laid out the escalating battle against the Marines. Start with the money argument, that America could make do without them on the grounds of helping the economy. The money argument would lead to the accusations of fraud and waste within the Marine Corps. The trail would then lead to the latest catastrophe, the killing of hundreds of Marines and the implications of a poorly-led military force.

Leaders in the other services were being asked for their opinions. While most snubbed reporters or simply offered their condolences for the Marines lost, there were a few who'd warmed to the idea of an armed forces without the Marine Corps. The anonymous sources from the Army said that they could just as easily fill in the void. They'd already been training on Navy amphibious vessels for years. One anonymous colonel said that amphibious landings themselves were a thing of the past, an outdated maneuver that the Marines still clung to out of stubborn pride. Sources from the Navy were saying that it didn't really matter who they ferried around on their fleets. While the Marines had always been a part of the

Navy way of life, why not try something new? It was, after all, the twenty-first century and the Army had the new technology that would complement the Navy's innovative platforms.

And so it went. Each piece would work off the other, feeding the whole, with the help of Steiner, the media and an enraged populace. It was a tsunami the Marine Corps could not avoid. Accusations would lead to investigations, which would lead to convictions and then the final nail in the Marine coffin, disbandment.

Weeks ago, the idea might've sounded ludicrous to all but the most liberal minded academics, but now opinion was shifting. There were too many questions to be ignored, too many implications for the thousands of young men and women who filled the Marine ranks each year. His office alone had already received over twenty letters from concerned parents whose children were either in Marine boot camp or had signed up to go. They wanted answers.

McKnight told himself that it was too late, the ball was already rolling. With a few more well-placed jabs, the Marine Corps would be left reeling against the ropes without the ability to defend itself.

That gave Congressman McKnight two options: 1) help deliver the death blow and place the blame in Zimmer's lap, or 2) swoop in as the savior and reap the rewards. Either way, he would win, and winning meant putting McKnight one giant step closer to living in the White House.

CHAPTER 29

"I wouldn't have believed it if I hadn't seen it with my own eyes," said Vince, scratching his snow white beard.

"I promised under an hour," said Cal, downing the rest of his coffee and throwing the cup in the trashcan next to the park bench they were sitting on.

"It was actually thirty-nine minutes exactly."

"I told you he was good."

"The best," added Gaucho, who was sitting across from them with Daniel and MSgt Trent.

"And you said you got him from the CIA?" asked Vince.

Cal nodded.

Vince whistled in admiration. "I sure would've liked to have had him on a couple recent ops. You ever loan him out?"

"Not if I can help it."

Vince shook his head. Cal was glad his team had so amazed the Delta commander. Gaucho had told Cal on the way out of Bragg that Vince was one of the best, a guy who was not only smart but one of the men. He'd apparently

160

spurned multiple attempts to be put behind a desk, for his career's sake, of course. "He'll never pick up a star because of it," Gaucho had said, "but I don't think he cares."

It seemed like a valid assessment to Cal. He wondered what would happen to the caliber of military officers if they weren't forced to take non-field assignment and allowed to choose their own path. Everyone always said it made both officers and enlisted more well-rounded, but what did that really mean? Cal put the thought off for another day and focused on the task at hand.

They were waiting for one of Vince's friends to show. The guy worked for a company called OrionTech, the place Bobby had said his buddy worked at as a security contractor. OrionTech had an office just outside of Ft. Bragg in Fayetteville for obvious reasons. If you're going to supply the military's elite, you might as well set up shop next to where they live.

"You ever worked with OrionTech, Vince?" Cal asked.

Vince nodded. "They've got some good engineers in the Fayetteville facility who specialize in next generation munitions and weaponry. Not the larger caliber stuff, but special operations and infantry grade. In exchange for our input, we get to keep the gear if we like it."

Cal knew the system well as his father's company, Stokes Security International, did the same thing. If you were in the business of building military technology, it was good to make friends with the services.

"What does the guy we're meeting do for OrionTech?"

"He's in upper level sales, but he used to be one of us. Keeps tabs on the other operators when he can. Converted over to the dark side when OrionTech offered him too much money to pass up. Good man."

They sat in silence until a man in a sharp suit appeared on the path and made his way over to them. He looked like any one of a thousand suits Cal had met in his lifetime. The man could've easily disappeared in a banker's convention.

"Vince," the man said, shaking his friend's hand.

"Rick Chapman, I'd like you to meet some of my friends."

Rick nodded to the others.

"I've got an eight o'clock, but you said it wouldn't take long."

"Just a couple of questions," said Vince. "I was hoping you could keep this between us."

"Of course."

"Good. I'll get right to it. Some guys who worked for OrionTech might've had something to do with the recent attacks on the Marines."

Rick frowned. "Well that's coming out of left field, even for you."

"I know, but we got the information from a pretty reliable source."

"Okay. How do you think I can help?"

"Have you ever heard of a couple two-stars by the names of—" Vince turned to Cal, who finished the question.

"Joseph Gower and Duane Mason?"

Rick's eyes registered recognition. "Admiral Gower?"

"Yeah. They both work at the Pentagon."

"I'm not supposed to know this, but Admiral Gower is on tap to be our new CEO."

Bingo, thought Cal. He'd decided to ask about Gower and Mason on a whim. The work Neil, Jonas and Diane were doing had yet to find anything out of the ordinary on the two flag officers.

"And Mason?"

Rick shook his head. "Doesn't ring a bell."

Two for two would've been too easy.

"What exactly does this have to do with the Marines?" asked Rick.

"That brings me to my second question," said Vince. "Have you heard any rumors about OrionTech employees who are former soldiers, Delta even, who've recently shipped overseas in small teams?"

"I don't think so. We have a small VIP protection division, but they base those guys out of another office."

Vince looked to Cal, who shrugged.

"That's all we wanted to know," said Vince. "And remember, keep this to yourself. It may be nothing, but we'll get to the bottom of it soon."

"No problem. Let me know if there's anything else you think I can help with. If there's a chance that some of our people had anything to do with what happened overseas—"

The rest of the men nodded. Rick understood.

Once they were back in Vince's beat up Aerostar van, they discussed the implications of what Gower's involvement could mean.

"Do you think he was the ringleader?" asked Gaucho.

"It's gotta be more than just coincidence," answered Cal. "We'll see if Neil can't work his magic and tap into OrionTech's system. Maybe that'll give us some answers."

No one said a word as Vince maneuvered through the early morning Fayetteville traffic. Cal wondered if Gower was simply using his contacts at OrionTech to wage his own personal war against the Marine Corps, or if OrionTech leadership was somehow involved. He didn't like either option, but going up against forces that had the backing of one of the world's largest military suppliers wasn't a good thought.

───────

Rick Chapman took the long way back to the office. It was a sunny morning and the sidewalks were scattered with joggers and power walkers. After doing a couple back and forths to make sure he hadn't been followed, Rick pulled out his cell phone and dialed a number from memory.

"Yes?"

"I have something for you."

"Go ahead."

"An old friend just stopped by to ask about you."

"And who would that be?"

"Vince Sweeney."

"The Delta commander."

"You remember?"

"Of course. Did he remember me?"

"No," answered Rick. "But he was with some friends."

"More Delta?"

"I don't think so. They didn't say."

"What did they say?"

"They asked about you and Gower."

"What did you tell them?"

"That I wasn't supposed to know that Gower was going to be our new CEO."

"And about me?"

"I said I didn't know you."

"Was that all?"

"No. They asked about any company operator's involvement with the Marine thing."

"And what did you say to that?"

"I told them I hadn't heard of anything, but that I'd keep an ear out."

There was a pause as the man on the other end of the line digested the information.

"Maybe we can use this. I'll be in touch."

There was a click and the call ended.

Rick replaced the phone in his pocket and continued toward his office. Who would've thought that such a juicy piece of intel could fall right into his lap? He wondered what Vince would think if he knew that his old friend was working for the very man they were looking for.

CHAPTER 30

Cal sighed and ended the call with Special Agent Barrett. The NCIS agent and his companion had yet to find anything in the Ellwood home, even after spending most of the night searching. They were going back soon to resume the haystack picking.

Cal thumbed through Gen. Ellwood's diary again. Other than the circled names and the note at the end, it didn't look like the former Assistant Commandant of the Marine Corps had left any clues. Just to be safe, Cal had instructed Mrs. Ellwood not to say a thing to either NCIS agent about the diary and the names it contained. Until he knew he could really trust Barrett, there was no need to leak information that they still hadn't proved to be of any real significance. He also didn't need the NCIS ringing the alarm and alerting Gower and Mason.

For his part, Barrett sounded like he was enjoying the laborious task of the painstaking search. Cal had to hand it to the guy, he was methodical and professional when the incentive was there. He wondered what Barrett would say if he found out that Cal had located a key piece of information and not shared it. He'd worry about that later. Surely he could figure out a way to give the NCIS agent his portion of credit.

"Anything from headquarters yet?" Cal asked Daniel, who'd volunteered to coordinate the efforts with Neil, Jonas and Diane. The sniper knew his boss was still a bit unsettled by his girlfriend's role in the operation. Better to keep the two apart for the time-being. Cal wouldn't say so, but he'd been relieved when Daniel had suggested splitting duties.

"Still a blank on Gower and Mason other than the fact they're both on leave. Neil says he's widening the net to include ports of entry. Maybe they went out of the country."

It was possible, but where would they go?

FALLS CHURCH, VIRGINIA
10:14AM

Barrett slid the thick book back into the tall bookshelf then grabbed another. His partner, Special Agent Weston Moore, was sifting through boxes of old Ellwood family photo albums.

Something about the monotonous drudgery of the task appealed to Barrett's senses. It was what he'd always imagined sleuths of another century doing, lifting every rock and analyzing every paper. Stokes hadn't told him what they might find, but the urgency in the Marine's instructions told Barrett that what they were doing could possibly be the key to unraveling the mystery of Gen. Ellwood's death.

Of course, it didn't hurt that the whole thing might get tied back to the sensationalized battle between Congressman Steiner and the Marine Corps. Not that Barrett really cared, other than for the horrific loss of American lives, but he couldn't believe the charade had gone on for so long. Surely the president or someone should have stepped in by then to do something.

But that was all way above Barrett's pay grade. His current focus had to do with finding clues. He thought about what Sherlock Holmes would do had he been in Barrett's shoes. Probably smoke a pipe or analyze the density and make of the bedroom carpets.

He chuckled to himself as he refocused on the task at hand, first holding the paperback book by the spine and leafing through the pages to see if anything fell to the floor. Nothing did. On to the tedious task of flipping from one page to the next. Not for the first time, he wondered why Stokes had told him to place the most emphasis on the books.

Weston Moore interrupted his thoughts when he walked into the library, his heels thumping on the rug covered hardwood floor.

"Nothing in the photo albums. Want me to help you in here?" Moore asked.

"I got to here," Barrett pointed to the empty spot on the bookshelf and swept his hand back over the area he'd already searched. "Why don't you start at the end and we'll meet in the middle."

"Got it."

Barrett was impressed by the new agent. The guy didn't complain about anything. He was an eager pupil and had quickly found how to make Barrett's job easier. Barrett wished all new NCIS employees had the same attitude. He wondered if that had anything to do with Moore's military background. For the most part, the men and women who joined NCIS from the armed services were used to putting in long hours and working hard to get things done. Moore was a shining example of what a stint in the Army could do to spit out a better human being.

Special Agent Barrett was half way through his most recent inspection when Moore asked, "Did Stokes have any new information?"

"He said they were chasing down some leads, but nothing concrete."

"You're sure he's giving you the full scoop?"

"I've got a pretty good BS detector, Moore. Stick around a while and you will, too."

Moore nodded and went back to his work. The familiar ringing of Moore's cell phone made Barrett look up in annoyance. He'd told the younger agent to put the phone on vibrate.

"Sorry," said Moore, answering the call. "Moore."

Barrett was only half listening when his partner said, "It's for you."

"That's strange," said Barrett. Moore stepped over and went to hand his superior the phone. But then he did something strange. Instead of putting it in Barrett's hand, he dropped it and came closer. Everything slipped to slow motion, the book falling out of Barrett's hand as his arms came up to block Moore, who was now grabbing the older agent by the back of the head. Before he knew what was happening, Moore's knee blasted into Barrett's sternum, causing him to double over, struggling to find breath.

He felt it when Moore slipped the pistol out of his side holster then kicked him from his knees onto his back. "Good night, Special Agent Barrett."

Robbie Barrett couldn't get his hands from his stomach to his head fast enough to block the descending blow from his own pistol butt. He felt a stab of pain on the side of his head, and then the world turned to black.

Special Agent Moore picked up his phone from the floor and made a call.

"What's your status?" asked the familiar voice.

"None so far," Moore replied.

"I know it's there. What about the wife and your partner?"

"She's tied up and he's unconscious."

"You don't think it's better to get rid of him?"

"I figured he might come in handy. I can always take care of him later."

There was what sounded like a growl from the other end. "You mean like you did in Florida?"

Moore took the jab without offering an excuse. "This time I've got him down."

"Okay. The wife is the key. Knock her around if you have to, but find out where he hid it."

"What if she doesn't know?" asked Moore.

"Even if she thinks she doesn't, he would've left a clue."

"So I'm supposed to get it out of her or keep digging here until I find it?"

"Is that a problem?"

Moore knew he was on shaky ground with his employer. He'd already failed twice in a matter of days. The man on the other end of the line wouldn't tolerate another slip up.

"It's not a problem. I'll take care of it."

"Good."

CHAPTER 31

Glen Whitworth sipped his third pina colada of the morning as he lounged in one of the water-filled floating rings in the small manmade lagoon. He rubbed his growing belly and let out a burp. He'd just eaten a late breakfast, but he was already thinking of lunch. Maybe a wood fired pizza, the one with the blue cheese.

He smiled and took another sip of his drink. While he could afford going to any resort in the world, something about coming to an all-inclusive appealed to Whitworth's frugal ways. He didn't have a problem paying hundreds of thousands to fund a politician's re-election campaign, or funneling millions into a company acquisition, but something about the effort of pulling out your wallet every time you wanted a drink annoyed him. Even worse, he hated the expectant look on waiters' faces when they wanted a hefty tip.

He never had to deal with that at Sandals. Everything was paid for and tips weren't technically allowed. Sure, he'd had to give Duane Mason the cash to pay the local thugs to dispose of Joe Gower's body, but that was business.

Part of him wanted to live on vacation all the time. If he'd really wanted to, he could. He could sell out of OrionTech or merely step aside. He had billions either way. But that would never work. Just like his father before him, Glen Whitworth knew he'd probably die of a heart attack as he worked another long day at OrionTech.

He couldn't complain. He loved the daily battles and the intrigue. He'd had more fun in this most recent scrap with the Marine Corps than any time since his hard-partying days in college. He wondered what the government would do with all that surplus military equipment once the Marines were dismissed. Probably sell it off for pennies on the dollar just like they'd done with all those MRAPs after Iraq wound down. Whitworth snorted. If it wasn't for the federal government and their constant churn of oversight, he would never have his billions. While the government moved from one crisis to another, appointing a new panel for this, then disbanding it and replacing it with something else, they never had any real consistency. With new development alone, there were not only new political appointees overseeing the programs, there were new admirals and generals who came and went every couple of years. It was easy to play the system and shuffle into a more favorable position once somebody left. It was like getting to reinvent yourself every two to three years.

His father had taught him how to bend the system and morph like a chameleon. The Whitworths were masters of reinvention. The billions of dollars in assets and cash were the proof.

A shrill whistle sounded from shore, jostling him from his thoughts. He rolled over with some effort, careful not to spill the remains of his cocktail, and saw Duane Mason standing on the white sand beach.

Whitworth held up his hand indicating he'd be there in a minute. After guzzling the rest of his drink, he splashed back into the water and ambled to shore. He couldn't wait to hear the latest from his newest enforcer.

***

CHARLOTTESVILLE, VIRGINIA
12:51PM

"Got it!" Neil shouted, almost knocking his Diet Red Bull onto the floor.

"What?" asked Diane, taking her eyes from the computer screen she'd been glued to all morning.

"I got into the U.S. Immigration system. Gower flew to Jamaica a couple days ago. His arrival documentation with the Jamaican authorities says he was going to the Sandals resort in Ocho Rios."

"Anything on Mason?" asked Diane.

"No, but they haven't recorded Gower's re-entry. That means he's still there."

Diane didn't disagree. She still wondered where Gen. Mason was. If anything, she would've thought they'd be together. With the help of Neil's computer skills (most of which she'd realized were highly illegal), they'd pieced together a rough history of both men and their association with Gen. Ellwood. From their time at the Naval Academy all the way up to present day, the three men had crossed paths on numerous occasions.

If Gower and Mason were behind Ellwood's death, Diane wondered what could have split the friendship so dramatically. The former Navy intel analyst knew that people changed and that priorities shifted over time, but for one of three college friends to end up on the business end of a pistol because of the other two, it was almost too much to believe. If she hadn't found her own proof concerning Cal, she might not have believed it. This was a new world for Diane. Could anyone be trusted?

"I haven't found any links with OrionTech," she offered. "Do you really think they're in on it too?"

Neil shrugged. "Cal seems to think so."

"And is Cal always right?"

Neil grinned. "Nine times out of ten."

Diane returned the smile. She was enjoying working with Cal's team. They were talented and obviously entranced by their work. These were guys who were doing the right thing, even if it was a bit outside the law. Diane's biggest immediate concern was for Cal. She couldn't shake the feeling that he was being led down a dangerous path. That message her friend had given her said it all. They wanted Cal dead.

She now knew that he was more than capable of protecting himself, but she wondered if he knew the breadth of what he'd stepped into. When you threw money and power into the winner's box, the stakes couldn't get much higher. And with the prize at the top so tantalizingly close, what crook wouldn't justify the means to the end?

Diane shook the morbid thoughts away. She had to look past the danger even if it meant ignoring the nagging fears for the man she loved. This was the reason why the military didn't let couples serve together. The proximity might seem like the perfect idea, but when you tossed in the possibility of harm coming to your loved one, the uncertainty of the situation only increased, putting the mission in peril.

Right now it had to be about the mission. Cal was a big boy. He could take care of himself. Or at least that's what Diane told herself as she dove into another long and convoluted government contract outlining OrionTech's latest bid to nab more federal billions. Neil was on the phone with Cal giving him the news about Gower's trip to Jamaica.

———◆———

FT. BRAGG, NORTH CAROLINA

"What do you think he's doing in Jamaica?" MSgt Trent asked. They'd all listened in on Cal's conversation with Neil, including Vince.

"Maybe he's really on vacation," said Cal.

"Seems like a funny time to hit the beach," offered Gaucho. "I mean, if the admiral's in the middle of this mess, shouldn't he be in town to run it?"

Cal shrugged. With technology the way it was, you could run a covert operation from anywhere. Terrorists across the globe were doing that very thing on a daily basis.

"Maybe we should pay him a visit," said Cal. "How long does it take to get there?"

"From here, probably about three and a half hours," offered Vince. "Depends on how fast your bird flies."

"Gaucho, would you mind calling the Powers brothers and have them plot the flight just in case?"

"No problem."

Gaucho moved off to call the TJG pilots while the others discussed how they could best capitalize on the information about Gower. A key piece was missing: General Mason. While Gower might've been at the helm of the conspiracy, Cal was starting to wonder if the man with special operations experience had been behind the attacks on the Marines. They needed to question Gower, but without spooking Mason. Their next task was pinpointing both of their whereabouts and seeing if they could all have a little chat.

Cal excused himself from the others and went to make a call. The Commandant would want to know how things were progressing now that the president had Congressman Steiner on lockdown for the foreseeable future. Cal and the Marine general knew they were getting close. The problem was, would the enemy go down swinging?

CHAPTER 32

With their business in Ft. Bragg concluded for the moment, The Jefferson Group had hopped back on their plane and landed at Reagan National just after 4pm. Vince was putting out some feelers with some friends he'd made in Jamaica during a cross-training the year before. He was confident that if Gower was still on the island, the Jamaicans could find him and keep tabs on the admiral. Vince had even volunteered to fly down there himself and apprehend Gower if that's what Cal needed.

They'd bide their time for now and see what the Jamaican authorities could find.

Diane and Neil had just arrived from Charlottesville, and Cal and his girlfriend were enjoying a quiet room service dinner in his hotel room. They'd been discussing OrionTech and the possible motives for the corporation to be involved in the latest dust-up.

"Are you sure you're okay with me being here?" Diane asked, sipping from a glass of house red. There'd been an awkward moment when she'd arrived, kind of like your family showing up at work when you were knee deep in the weeds. Happy to see them, but distracted.

"I'll get used to it," Cal answered honestly. They'd take it a step at a time just like they had with their romantic relationship. Diane would be starting the new semester in January, so the arrangement might not even be a permanent thing. Part of him hoped it wouldn't be. He knew how he could be on the job, especially in the middle of an operation, and that wasn't something he wanted Diane to see.

"Just tell me if I'm in the way and I'll scoot to the side. Really, Cal, I understand that this is your thing. I don't want my being here to come between us."

She understood him so well.

"As long as you promise that you'll forgive me for losing my temper every once in a while."

"Deal," she said, sticking out her hand. He grabbed it and pulled her out of her chair and onto the couch. She plopped down with a laugh. "What time do you have to go?"

"I told Mrs. Ellwood that Daniel and I would be there around six."

"That should give us plenty of time."

"Time for…?"

He grinned when he saw the lascivious look in her eyes.

"Don't worry, I'll make sure you're on time."

"Oh?" Cal asked, pulling her closer.

"Yeah," she whispered. "I hate unpunctual men."

Daniel pulled their new rental in next to what must have been Barrett's rental car. Cal hadn't spoken to the NCIS agent all day, but he assumed Barrett would've called if he'd found anything.

He knocked on the front door and was surprised to see the young agent they'd first encountered on their trip to Orlando days before. Cal couldn't remember the guy's name.

"Mr. Stokes, good to see you again," said the agent.

"I'm sorry. I never got your name."

"I'm Weston Moore. I guess you could call me Robbie's flunky."

He led them into the house as they spoke.

"Are you new with NCIS?" asked Cal.

"Yeah. Been with them less than a year."

"Former military?"

"Army, but don't hold that against me."

Moore seemed like a nice guy. Cal saw that he still had his coat and tie on. He would've thought they'd dressed down a bit considering the boring task he and Barrett had been relegated to.

"So where's Barrett?"

"He and Mrs. Ellwood stepped out to pick up some dinner. She's really made us feel at home."

"She's a nice lady," said Cal.

"She is," replied Moore, showing them into Gen. Ellwood's office. "Well, here's what we've examined so far."

Moore gave them a rundown of everything they'd done. Cal was impressed. Barrett had taken the chore seriously, really gone to it with a fine tooth comb.

"Sounds like you've got it covered. Thanks again for your help on this. I can imagine you'd probably rather be doing something else," offered Cal.

"All Robbie had to say was that this might help crack the case with the whole Marine thing. I can't tell you how sorry I am for your loss."

"Thanks," Cal said. The guy was laying it on pretty thick. Maybe he was just trying to get in their good graces. Who knew what Barrett had told the guy?

"Hey, you guys want anything to drink? Mrs. Ellwood made some tea that is really dynamite."

"Sure, I'll have some."

Daniel nodded too.

———

Special Agent Weston Moore walked into the kitchen and grabbed a tray from the countertop. He then filled two glasses with ice tea and set them on the tray, along with a pile of napkins. Moore took a steadying breath, imagining the scope on his favorite rifle, waiting to be given the green light to fire downrange.

He slipped his pistol out of his pocket and held it underneath the tray. It took him a second to get it positioned just right, but then he had it set. As long as he kept it at waist level the two Marines would never see it.

A smile made its way to his face as he entered the office again. Stokes and Briggs were scanning some files that Moore had set out for them to peruse.

"Anything interesting?" he asked, gauging his distance, wanting to be perfectly prepared to take the shots.

"Not really. You guys are probably better at this anyway."

"I don't know about that. Here's your tea," said Moore, extending the tray toward Stokes.

"You can just put it on the desk," said Stokes, not lifting his head from his reading.

Moore hesitated. His targets weren't where he wanted them. As he tried to figure out what to do, his eyes locked on Briggs. The sniper had somehow changed. Gone was the passivity Moore had thought looked more like boredom. No. Now the man's eyes held recognition, a hardness Moore had seen on the battlefield, when a combatant recognizes the enemy.

The tray slipped from his hand and Moore was in the process of turning his wrist so he could properly aim when Briggs's foot connected with his shooting hand. The weapon fired as Moore wondered how Briggs had reacted so quickly. Surprise turned to horror as the blond sniper he'd been so eager to kill moments earlier, now loomed before him, pistol extended, aim steady, right at Moore's face.

He considered fighting it out. Maybe he could take one of them down before he was killed. But instead, he dropped his weapon to the ground, his hand involuntarily raising in the air.

By now Stokes had his weapon out, too. "Get on your knees."

Moore obeyed, eyeing both men with the contempt that was now crackling in his stomach. He'd been so close. How had Briggs…

"Where are Barrett and Mrs. Ellwood?" Stokes asked, stepping closer.

"Fuck you."

Stokes's boot caught him in the stomach. Moore couldn't help doubling over.

"Let me guess, you're the asshole that tried to take us out the other day," said Stokes.

Moore didn't answer, still trying to catch his breath.

"Who are you?" asked Briggs, his voice like a snake who'd wrapped its prey in its coils and now had all the time in the world to get the answers it needed.

Moore got back to his knees and said, "Sergeant Weston E. Moore, United States Army. Sniper." He spat the last word out like a dagger. If the designation registered with Briggs, he didn't show it.

"You were the one in Florida," Briggs said. Moore could almost see the pieces clicking together in the Marine's head.

"Where's Gower?" Stokes asked.

Moore didn't take his eyes from Briggs. It would've been so sweet to put a bullet into the man's forehead. When he'd found out that Briggs had been up for the Medal of Honor, but that the award was pulled at the last minute, Moore knew he'd found his prize. The legacy of sniper on sniper warfare went back generations. The fact that Briggs was part of the cocky Marine brotherhood would've only made it more delectable.

Stokes was speaking, but Moore didn't hear. Images floated across his conscious mind. He'd been imprisoned before. His spotter dead and his unit out of reach, the Taliban had found him after a bloody fight. He'd taken down at least twenty, but then his ammunition had run out, and there were just too many of them. Weeks of torture. Nights of horror. He wouldn't let that happen again.

The only man who hadn't left him to die was General Mason. He'd found out about the sniper's capture and committed every troop he had to get him back. It took months, but finally Sgt. Moore was rescued. He came out of it a broken man. Once sure of his abilities, everything now seemed wrong.

Gen. Mason took a special interest in him, ensuring he had the best treatment for his physical as well as his mental disabilities. It took time, but he'd made it back. He'd proven that he still had it. Moore hadn't pulled the trigger for Gen. Ellwood, but sure would have if the Marine hadn't had the courage.

And now here he was again, on the wrong side of the barrel. But this time he was at peace. It wasn't that he didn't care, but he'd come prepared. It only took a subtle shift, scraping his back teeth together as he'd practiced so many times, like a fine trigger pull. He gave Briggs a wink, and clamped his teeth together.

Special Agent Moore crumbled to the floor, his head slamming against the corner of the large wood desk. Cal watched him fall, thinking that the spy was putting on a ruse. He hadn't seen the wink.

"He's dead," said Daniel, bending down to check for a pulse.

"What?"

"He had an L-pill." L-pills, also known as kill-pills, had been improved since the early days of cyanide filled capsules.

They'd at one time considered issuing a CIA version of the pill to the TJG operators, but the entire team had refused, opting to take the chance of capture rather than to take their own lives.

Daniel closed his eyes and mouthed a silent prayer. Cal didn't join in, leaving the task to his more spiritual friend.

Once he was finished, Daniel stood up and said, "Let's go find Mrs. Ellwood."

They found Special Agent Barrett drugged in a small guest room bathtub. Other than a nasty welt on his head, he looked okay.

Cassidy Ellwood was in the master walk-in closet. She'd been worked over by Moore and sported a black eye, swollen lip and some bruised ribs. Despite her injuries, Mrs. Ellwood looked more relieved than frightened.

"We need to get you to the hospital, Mrs. Ellwood," said Cal, upset that he'd let harm come to the grieving widow.

"That can wait," she replied, wiping her face with a wet washcloth as she examined herself in the bathroom mirror.

"Ma'am, we really should get you to a more secure location."

"Don't you want to debrief me first?"

She sounded like an exhausted Marine who'd just come in off patrol. Cal hadn't expected the question.

"There's time for that later. Right now—"

"Mr. Stokes, if it means getting closer to the bastards who killed my husband, I'd appreciate you getting that information right now." Like before, she said it with the authority that only a general's wife could wield.

"Okay. Tell me what happened."

"I won't bore you with the details. The most important thing is that he kept asking for something. He thought I knew where it was."

"And do you?"

"I don't even know what he wanted. He said Doug hid it and my life depended on him finding it. Honestly, other than the diary I gave you, I don't have a clue what he was looking for."

So there was something. A puzzle piece that the enemy wanted. Maybe Gen. Ellwood had left behind an insurance policy. Cal would need more help if they were going to find it.

"Tell you what, let me get someone over here to take a look at you, Mrs. Ellwood. I'll also bring over some friends who can keep an eye on the place and help find whatever the other side is looking for."

Mrs. Ellwood smiled. "That's better."

CHAPTER 33

He'd slipped out of Jamaica just in time. No sooner had the Whitworth's jet left the deck, than his local contacts called to inform him that Jamaican authorities were poking around, asking about Gower. They'd found his girlfriend and were in the process of threatening her with jail time unless she told them what they wanted to know.

Gen. Mason chuckled. The woman didn't know anything. Gower had brought her along for an easy lay. The guy had never had the confidence to fish for someone out of his league, so he'd always poached on ogling staffers who appreciated the attention of a decent looking Navy man.

His office was covered with messages and files. It would take him a day to shuffle the work out to his underlings. He'd perfected the art of delegating administrative tasks. Being part of the Pentagon's procurement apparatus meant more than a little paperwork, but within months of assuming his final post, Mason had his system set.

From the day he'd stepped in the windowless office, he planned for his retirement. There were plenty of companies who would love to hire a two-star general, but most of the offers he'd considered seemed beneath him.

Joe Gower had been the key. Over the years Mason had always been content with allowing his former roommate to take the lead. It made Gower happy, and despite the occasional haughty comment, it made him bearable. What Gower didn't know was that Mason was always watching. He'd learned to manipulate his Academy classmate in a hundred different ways. Proud people were like that. Give them incentive or prod them with compliments and there wasn't much you couldn't get them to do.

But Gower was the one who'd had initial contact with OrionTech and Glen Whitworth. He'd formed the relationship and put his own neck on the line while Mason nudged him forward. Gower had even introduced Mason to Whitworth, and the two men had formed an instant connection. For months they'd schemed behind Gower's back. The look on the admiral's face had said it all as his supposed friend had taken his life. Gower hadn't suspected.

It was what Mason was good at. The service taught you to be a chameleon. Sometimes you had to kiss a little ass and sometimes you had to kick some. Mason figured that he probably could've picked up another star if he'd wanted to, but by the time he'd met Whitworth, he'd gotten bored with the Army. Training had thrilled him and combat had fueled him. But those days were gone. Now all he had to look forward to was getting old and being some sort of worthless figurehead. Glen Whitworth had changed all that.

Whitworth wanted to revolutionize the military supply chain for the 21st century. He wanted OrionTech weapons in the hands of every soldier, sailors cruising the Persian Gulf on OrionTech ships and Air Force pilots flying OrionTech jets. He already had an impressive foothold, but he wanted more. Mason could relate.

While Whitworth wanted to wine and dine the political elite, Mason wanted to be with the troops, smell the briny ocean and feel the downdraft of a lifting chopper. It was a perfect match. While Whitworth stepped out of his role as CEO and redoubled his efforts on Capitol Hill, Mason could focus on his public role as CEO to help the troops. It didn't hurt that he'd be making millions in the process.

So to Mason, the marriage with Whitworth and OrionTech was as close to a four leaf clover that he'd ever found. He could go on experiencing the thrill of military life while earning a very comfortable living.

He was thinking of all these things when he heard a knock on his door.

"Come," he said reluctantly.

His secretary poked her head inside. "General, I have someone here who would like to speak with you."

"I told you I needed the day. No meetings," he replied.

"But, sir, the gentleman has a letter from the Commandant of the Marine Corps himself."

That got Mason's attention.

"What does he want?"

"He said he'd been instructed to ask for your assistance with their latest…problems."

It was too good. The very entity he was trying to crush was coming to him for help.

"Please show him in."

The secretary disappeared and a moment later a young man in a button down shirt and sport coat walked in. He looked vaguely familiar, but Mason couldn't place him. The door was pulled closed by his secretary, who retreated back to her desk.

"How can I help the Marine Corps today, Mr....?"

"You don't need to know my name, General."

Mason scowled.

"I was prepared to assist you in any way I could, but if you insist on being—"

"Cut the crap, General. Think a little harder and you'll figure out why I'm here."

Mason stared at the man and recognition finally slapped him in the face.

"You're Stokes." He'd only seen an out of focus picture of the man that Weston Moore had sent him, but he was sure.

Stokes smiled. "The Commandant has asked me to escort you to his office."

Mason's unease fell away. "Tell me why."

"First, I'm sure he'd like to have a chat. And second, the MPs will be waiting to throw you behind bars."

"And why would that be, Mr. Stokes? What is it that I don't know?"

"I'm sure you know plenty. Gower. Dead Marines. OrionTech."

"I don't know what you're talking about. Let's turn the tables, shall we? It's obvious by your lack of entourage that you have no evidence. You're pulling the old 'Marine charge the hill routine,' right? See if General Mason will admit to something he didn't do. Well that's not going to happen. You can tell Winfield that I'm not coming."

Stokes didn't move. In fact, he didn't show a flicker of alarm. "I probably shouldn't tell you this, but Congressman Steiner is in FBI custody."

Mason's stomach lurched, but he kept his face neutral. "Why should that bother me?"

"I have a feeling that the FBI is about to find out that you and Gower are somehow attached to Steiner's report."

"You think I would be stupid enough to be a source for him, even anonymously?" Mason laughed. "Maybe Joe Gower is that stupid, but not me, boy."

"And where is Admiral Gower? Still at the Sandals resort in Ocho Rios, Jamaica?"

Mason crossed his arms over his chest. "If you have an issue with Joe Gower, I suggest you take it up with him." It was good to know that the Jamaicans had done their job properly. Nobody would ever see Gower again.

Stokes shrugged as if he didn't care.

"We'll find him in time, I'm sure. But you're the one I really want, General. I have a feeling that you were the one that had our Marines killed. We're close to having everything. And when we do, you and your men are going down."

Stokes headed for the door. Mason had to give it to the kid, he had some balls marching into the Pentagon and confronting an Army general. He wondered who this Stokes guy really was and how he'd gotten close to the Commandant. That gave him an idea.

"I have a deal for you," said Mason.

Stokes turned to face him. "Unless it's a full confession, I really don't have time."

"What if I told you that you could get everything you want? Gower. The operatives behind the attacks. Everything."

"And what do I have to do to get that?"

Mason stood up from his desk.

"Are you a student of history, Stokes?"

Stokes nodded.

"Are you familiar with the tradition of gentleman's duels?"

Another nod.

"I was thinking that we could do the same."

"Why?"

"Well, you come barging into my office, questioning my honor. Shouldn't I have the chance to defend myself?"

"So you want to go outside, stand back to back, take ten paces, and then see who can kill the other?"

"No. I had something more…entertaining in mind. I assume that you have a team at your disposal? One that has seen the flash of enemy gunfire and experienced the glory of battle?"

Stokes frowned.

"I'll take that as a yes," said Mason, warming to his idea. "I propose a gentleman's duel. My team versus your team. I choose the location and the method by which we fight, and if you win, you get my confession and everyone who helped me."

"Is this what you do all day, concoct moronic ways to pretend you're still on the front lines?"

The jab hurt Mason more than he would've expected.

"I've shed more blood for this country than you ever will," he replied.

Stokes grinned. "I doubt that, but let's assume I don't go along with your cowboys and Indians game. What happens then?"

It was Mason's turn to grin. "If you don't agree to my terms, there will be more horrific attacks on your beloved Marine brethren."

CHAPTER 34

General Winfield listened as Cal delivered a summary of his encounter with General Mason. He had a half a mind to call the man himself, or better yet, send a platoon to pluck him out of his hiding spot and drag him to jail.

"I can't believe you're considering this, Cal. The man is deranged."

"I don't know how to explain it, general, but I think he's all there."

"So you think he'll put up his hands and surrender if we win this stupid game?"

"Isn't it worth a shot if it'll save Marine lives?"

"We've already got our units on high alert. If we somehow—"

"I don't think that will help. As much as I hate to say it, they really did a number on us before. To wipe out two companies without us knowing? They've got friends we haven't even seen yet."

"That's what makes me think that this whole idea is one big diversion. Come find me in the woods while I take a few more pieces out of the Marine Corps's foundation. It stinks, Cal. Don't you see that?"

Cal nodded. "I'm not saying it's perfect. God knows it's not. But if I can take a small team in, you're still free to use whatever resources you need to exploit the situation on your end."

"But we don't have anything."

"I have a feeling that General Ellwood left something for us to find. Mrs. Ellwood said that Moore kid was pretty hyped up about it. Why else would he kill himself with an L-pill?"

Gen. Winfield didn't have an answer. From the start of the whole affair he'd secretly blamed Doug Ellwood for the entire mess. Consciously or not, the man had erred. What would have happened if Ellwood had never been involved? But that was a moot point. It was done. They had what they had.

At every turn it seemed like the enemy was three steps ahead. Yes, the president had turned the tables on Steiner, but a new cloud had just appeared on the horizon, one that could possibly decimate more of his Marines.

Maybe Cal was right. Maybe they should take a chance. He saw now more than ever why the president put such trust in the young man. It reminded the crusty veteran that the United States had been founded by men the same age as Cal. What did that say for his aging generation?

"As long as it's all volunteers, I'll go along with your decision," said Winfield, hoping that he wouldn't come to regret his decision. Was he just sending five more men off to their deaths?

C. G. COOPER

Stokes nodded. "Don't worry, sir, it's the only way we operate."

They exchanged grim smiles, each already planning for their own contingencies.

9:57AM

Gen. Mason almost couldn't contain his excitement. Stokes had agreed to his proposal, and that meant that the Commandant was on board too. This was what he liked. Head to head. Nothing held back. Only the strong would survive.

Of course, he would have to stack the deck in his favor as much as he could. With the help of OrionTech's assets that wouldn't be a problem. After all, what good commander didn't utilize all the weapons in his arsenal?

FALLS CHURCH, VIRGINIA
10:15AM

Even though there was plenty of security at the house, Mrs. Ellwood answered the door.

"I'm Neil Patel, Mrs. Ellwood." Neil stepped to the side so that Diane could introduce herself.

"I'm Diane Mayer, Ma'am."

The two women shook hands.

"Thank you both for coming. Let me show you to my husband's office."

196

Neil had suggested to Cal that he scour the Ellwood computers for anything that might help the investigation. While Cal doubted that they held whatever Moore had been looking for (surely that's the first place Gower and Mason would've looked), he'd agreed because they'd run into a dead end with Admiral Gower. It was like the guy had been swept from the planet by a cosmic backhand. None of Neil's techy intrusions had managed to come up with a hint of his whereabouts, and the Jamaican authorities were still searching.

Even though it might be a lost cause, Cal had agreed because there wasn't much else for Neil to do. While most of their operations necessitated Neil's assistance, whether through some new gadgetry or hacking, this go-around would be different. Mason had been clear. No electronic gear. Except for the helo they'd be flying in on, they'd be doing it old school. Rifles and non-electronic gear were fine, but anything else was off limits.

"We'll have ways of knowing whether you follow the rules," Mason had said. "If you don't, the deal's off."

The guy was an egomaniac, but Cal didn't doubt the soldier's ability to turn on a dime. Best to follow the program and win on their own terms.

Diane had come along both to help Neil if needed, and to give a little female companionship to Mrs. Ellwood. The general's wife was smart enough to understand that the presence of her friends or daughters-in-law was impossible. She'd even seemed pleased when Cal made the suggestion.

"Another woman in the house might do wonders," Mrs. Ellwood had said.

Diane liked Cassidy Ellwood immediately. Despite everything that she'd been through, she held herself with a strength that Diane could not help but admire. She hoped that her being there would help.

"Is there anything I can do for you, Mrs. Ellwood?" Diane asked as they left Neil in the office.

"Yes. First, you can stop calling me Mrs. Ellwood. My first name Cassidy, but my friends call me Cassy."

"Okay, Cassy. Was there a second request?"

"Yes. You can tell me how long you and Cal have been dating."

Diane blushed.

"Oh, I don't mean to embarrass you, honey. And before you ask, no, he didn't tell me."

"Then how did you know?"

Cassy shrugged. "It was the way he talked about you. It's not the first time I've seen a Marine in love."

Diane smiled. "Was it the same for you and General Ellwood?"

Cassy Ellwood gave a small shrug and girlish smile. "Why don't you come into the kitchen. I'll make us up some coffee, and then I'll tell you about the pitfalls of falling in love with a Marine."

CHAPTER 35

"How long do you think this guy's gonna keep us in the air?" MSgt Trent asked over the pounding rotors of the MV-22B Osprey that the Commandant had loaned them. Cal had insisted they find their own transport, but Gen. Winfield was adamant.

"If I'm going to send you into combat, you'll be flying in on a Marine bird."

Thankfully they had accepted the Commandant's offer because they'd been flying in circles for hours. Mason had given Cal a rough outline of where they should loiter, but the large area gave them no clue as to their final destination. The crooked general was supposed to call when he and his men were in position. Then, and only then, would Cal have the coordinates of the objective. Mason said they were free to pick any insertion point they wanted, but that they had until midnight to conduct their final attack.

That would make things more than a little tricky. Mason and his men knew the land. Cal's team would have minutes to analyze the location, come up with a drop off point, plot an ingress route, and coordinate their attack plans.

On the positive side, he had some of the best with him. Daniel had volunteered first. He'd come armed with his M40 Sniper rifle rather than the bulkier .50 caliber Barrett. MSgt Trent and Gaucho were next, inseparable as always.

The last two members of their team of six had come as a surprise, and at the recommendation of Gaucho. Rather than bring two of his own men, he'd called back to Ft. Bragg. Vince and Karl had agreed on the spot, eager to deliver some payback to the corrupted soldiers.

Six men against who knew what. No electronics. No explosives other than grenades. Steel and flesh.

Mason had promised that other than the presence of highly advanced anti-air batteries that would keep Cal's supporters from bringing in close air support, he and five men would be under the same rules as their opponents.

And so they flew and they waited, watching the treetops below and wondering when the wheel would stop turning.

3:49PM

"You all know where to go."

The men around Mason nodded. They were pros. All they needed was a point in the right direction and off they went. If their success against the Marines was any indication, the men in the empty Quonset hut were the best of the best. Sure they'd had their run-ins with the law, some even spending time in the stockade and/or civilian jail, but when it came to taking out a target, there were few to rival their talent.

Mason had collected them over the years, helping them when no one else would. In return they'd pledged their loyalty as he'd stuffed their pockets with crisp dollar bills. The big payoff was coming. They'd struck the heart of their enemy, but the lumbering beast wasn't through yet. The operators salivated as much as their patron when they thought about the destruction of the Marine Corps and the spoils that would inevitably come their way.

The only tiny thing they had to do now was kill six idiots who were dumb enough to come onto their home turf. To the six men prepping their gear before step-off, the game was tailor-made.

<hr />

4:03PM

Cal wrote down the coordinates as Mason rattled them off. He repeated them to the general, who confirmed that they were correct.

The six men in the back of the Osprey examined the outspread map as the pilot shifted course toward their objective.

"At least he picked a spot away from civilization," said Trent.

He was right. There was nothing but trees, hills and rivers all around the objective.

They didn't want to insert too far away considering their time constraints and the terrain. It took them another two minutes to find a spot suitable for landing, and plot a preliminary ingress route.

Cal gave the pilot the LZ coordinates. After inputting them in his computer, the pilot said, "Seven Mikes."

Despite the situation, Diane had enjoyed her time with Cassy Ellwood. The stories she told about her time as a Marine wife made her want to laugh and cry. Cassy described her first date with her husband, and how he'd almost driven them off a cliff when he'd forgotten to put the borrowed convertible in park. She'd told Diane about the long deployments and the unknown. The retelling was her way of stepping back in time and walking in her old shoes. At times she laughed and once she cried when she told Diane about the baby she'd lost when then Col. Ellwood was on deployment.

"I never really forgave him for that," she'd said. Diane could understand. In a way it felt like a subtle warning. "Get mixed up with a Marine and this could happen to you."

But Diane appreciated Cassy's candid storytelling. She could tell that the career Marine wife wasn't sugar-coating a thing. Diane wondered if she would've done the same if she were in Cassy's shoes. In many ways, Cal's choice of career was even worse than General Ellwood's. Where at least Mrs. Ellwood knew basically where her husband was, and that he was surrounded by a battalion of Marines, Cal was the opposite. The Jefferson Group worked in small teams, often without outside help. Like they were doing now.

Diane wished she knew what was happening, but another part of her didn't. Would she be able to handle Cal's death as stoically as Cassy had with her husband? Diane doubted it.

And so she busied herself with helping Neil, then coming back to talk more with their hostess. They'd finally gotten to the end of the story. Cassy was telling Diane about their trip to Disney World.

"I pray that whoever you end up with, Diane, always strive to love each other as much as humanly possible. It may not be easy, but it will be worth it. I loved Doug despite his obsession for the Marine Corps. I know it was hard for him. He didn't understand our sons, who were more than a little rambunctious with their liberal stands. I don't blame him for pushing them away, just as they did to him. But there comes a point when a woman has to put her foot down. I gave him the choice, his family or his career." Cassy sighed. "If I'd only known what he was going through. If only he'd told me, maybe I could've helped. Maybe we could have run away and left it all behind."

Diane placed her hand on top of Cassy's.

"If I've learned anything about your husband today, it's that he wasn't afraid of a fight. I'm sure he found a way to hit back."

"And that's why you've all been searching the house, to see what he left behind?"

"Yes, Ma'am," Diane said, hurting for the woman who stared at her with tear-filled eyes, begging for a solution that Diane could not supply.

"So tell me about Disney. What did you do? What did you see?"

Cassy nodded and talked about how the trip had started off with its rocky moments, especially between General Ellwood and his sons, but that they'd warmed to him by the third day.

"And what about you and the general? Did you have time together?"

Cassy smiled, her eyes sparkling. "Selfishly, I think that was the best part. It was like we were dating again. He rarely let go of my hand. We stayed up late and slept in until room service came knocking. We talked like we hadn't talked in ages. I cared for him before we went, but I fell back in love with him while we were there. He really was like a college kid again. Nervous and horny. I thought he was having a seizure when he gave me my present."

"What did he give you?"

Mrs. Ellwood slipped a silver chain out of her blouse. On the end was a beautifully carved silver Eagle, Globe and Anchor with an impressive diamond set in the globe.

"I know it may seem cheesy, like a lance corporal giving his date a brass EGA, but the way he explained it to me…I don't think I'll ever take it off."

"What did he say?"

"Well, Doug wasn't much of a romantic, and he stumbled a bit before he found the right words, but the gist of it was that he found me and the Marine Corps at the same time, and that while I may think that he considered the Corps more than his own wife, the diamond signified our love, and that the answer to any of our questions always came back to that, love."

"Can I see it?" asked Diane.

Cassy smiled, unclasped it from her neck, and handed it to Diane. It was heavier than it looked. Not silver, probably platinum. The craftsmanship was superb with tiny intricate etchings along the eagle's wings and the contours around the globe. She turned it over, admiring the continued design on the back. Something got her attention. It looked like a little clasp, just barely noticeable.

"Is it a locket?" Diane asked.

"I don't think so, why?"

"It looks like there's a clasp, or maybe…"

Diane tried to slide her nail under it but it wouldn't give. She pressed harder and suddenly a perfectly inlaid hatch opened, like a secret door.

"What is it?" Cassy asked, breathless.

"There's something in it." Diane dumped the contents into her palm. It was a flat brown square with silver grooves that looked like a maze or railroads tracks crisscrossing at right angles. Her eyebrows jumped. "I think I know what it is!"

"What? What is it, Diane?"

"I think it's a microchip."

CHAPTER 36

They disembarked as quickly as they could, taking up positions, weapons ready. The pilot didn't waste any time. As soon as the last man had taken a knee, the Osprey powered up into the sky and disappeared over the trees.

Cal half expected the bird to be shot from the sky, and had recommended to the pilot that he loiter no longer than needed. The Marine captain and his co-pilot didn't need convincing. They were brave, but they weren't stupid.

As the sound of the hybrid Marine aircraft faded in the distance, Cal and his men watched and listened. Nothing. They waited another two minutes. Still nothing. The familiar racing blood coursed through Cal's veins, heightening his senses. He could smell the frozen ground through the cut of the winter chill.

Finally, when no surprise jumped out to greet them, the team split into teams of two. Daniel would take his customary role on point with a decent head start. Karl had volunteered to go with him since he had the most experience as a spotter. They moved off into the gloom with a quick nod.

Gaucho and Trent would take the easternmost route while Cal and Vince would take a westerly route. The three pairs would be walking in a rough triangle, dispersement being the key. Better to give Mason multiple targets than to stay clumped together. It was a risk, but an acceptable one.

Five minutes after Daniel and Karl had left, the others split off to make their way to the object, and Cal wondered what tricks they'd find along the way.

———◆———

4:13PM

"Sir, their aircraft just dropped them off and is making its way north."

"Good," replied Gen. Mason, who was wearing a set of fatigues he'd purchased before the first Gulf War. He hated the new digital patterns the Army had adopted, for once following suit behind the Marines. "Which LZ did they choose?" There weren't a lot of options for helicopter to land in the area he'd provided Stokes. Five had been pegged as the most likely to be used.

"They chose LZ Foxtrot, sir."

So they'd chosen the northern-most of the five. It was a smart move, giving the invading force the most space to work with, but it was farther to travel. Mason wondered whether Stokes's team of six would stick together or split. Not that it mattered, his men could handle either scenario, but something told him that they would maintain some sort of cohesion.

Mason had taken the opposite approach. His men were lone wolves, accustomed to working on their own. They thrived on it, mostly because they were more than a little rough around the edges, making teamwork challenging.

"Stow the laptop in my office and head out," Mason ordered, pulling one of three cigars out of his blouse pocket.

Dan did as instructed, and then left the warehouse a minute later, not even giving his commander a second glance. The others were exceptional, but Dan was the best Mason had. Sure, he had a cocaine problem and liked to slap girls around, but Dan was exactly what Mason needed, a ruthless killer who would stop at nothing to destroy the enemy. He never complained and always got the job done. The perfect weapon for taking down the United States Marine Corps.

FALLS CHURCH, VIRGINIA
4:32PM

Neil confirmed Diane's assessment and was in the process of digging out tools from one of his bags.

Diane and Cassy watched the perfectly tailored genius as he mumbled to himself and arranged his things neatly on the kitchen table.

"This may take a minute," he said when he finally looked ready to start his examination. "Every chip is made differently, and sometimes it's a matter of cracking the code, so to speak."

He adjusted his glasses, grabbed a set of fine tweezers and laid the chip on a glass slide under a portable microscope. Neil turned on the light source and looked through the eyepiece. After fine tuning the magnification, he said, "Looks like...hmm, I think this is a standard medical microchip."

"What does that mean?" asked Mrs. Ellwood.

Neil answered without looking up from his work. "It's a lot like the microchips they've been putting into pets for years, but now they have them for humans. They're implanted just under the skin and contain a sixteen digit ID number. The code is linked to a database that holds the patient's medical information, allergies, anything that could help medical professionals in the case that the person with the implant becomes incapacitated."

"Why would my husband use that?"

"They're fairly common and readily available. And they're not limited to medical history. You could put almost any information on them you'd like."

"Do you think he left us a message?"

"There's only one way to find out," said Neil. He grabbed a small wand from the desk, turned it on, and waved it over the microchip. A long number popped up on Neil's laptop. "I already know the manufacturer," he murmured as he clicked through screens, "So now all I need to do is tap into their medical database and...here it is."

Diane and Cassy leaned down to read what was on the computer screen.

Cassy, when you find this, take it straight to Scotty. He'll know what to do. Love, Doug

C. G. COOPER

Cassy Ellwood inhaled as Neil clicked through to the next section of the record. Diane's heart leapt. "Oh my…"

"Everything's here," interrupted Neil. "All the answers we've been looking for. Names, dates, connections, accounts."

Suddenly, Diane's vision blurred as reality stung. She grabbed the desk for support.

"Are you okay?" asked Neil.

Diane couldn't breathe, but she was able to choke out, "If everything's there, then Cal…"

"Oh shit," said Neil, the color draining from his face. "We need to call them back. But how? They don't have a radio or anything."

It was the general's wife who finally spoke through the shock. "We need to call Scotty Winfield."

———————

HEADQUARTERS MARINE CORPS
ARLINGTON, VIRGINIA
4:48PM

Gen. Winfield took notes as he listened to Cal's girlfriend recite what they'd learned. "And you're sure everything's there?" he asked.

"Yes, sir. There's even a note addressed to you. Would you like me to read it?"

"That can wait, Ms. Mayer. Would it be possible to bring everything here?"

"Yes, sir," she replied, a hint of panic in her voice.

"Don't worry, Ms. Mayer. I'll do everything I can to get Cal back."

"Thank you."

"No, Ms. Mayer, thank you."

The Commandant hung up the phone and walked out of his office. He knew what he needed to do.

CHAPTER 37

They were making good time. Daniel figured they'd be in position just before nine o'clock. He and Karl had passed an impressive anti-aircraft pod a few minutes earlier, the modern weapon humming with electricity. Karl had pointed out the OrionTech logo proudly displayed on its side. Other than the AA platform, they hadn't encountered any surprises.

The sniper was getting a feel for the terrain, starting to understand its subtle nuances. They'd found spent shell casings and the occasional blasted tree. Daniel had been on a lot of training facilities, from Twentynine Palms to the desert live fire ranges in Qatar. This was another one, Mason's playground.

Daniel crept up the slope of a tall rise, hoping to get a glimpse of what lay ahead. Night vision would've been nice, but luckily the night was clear and bright, the moon almost full as it cast down its pallor. He took cover behind a large cedar, scanning the area first with his naked eye and then raising his rifle to look through its scope.

Nothing visible, just the tops of trees and the many rises dotting the terrain. He took his time backing down the hill where he rejoined Karl.

"Anything?" asked Karl.

"Lots of trees," replied Daniel.

"I'll take point for the next stretch, if you want."

"I'm good."

They both froze when a branch snapped in the direction they were about to go. Rifles at the ready, they waited. Nothing came. Daniel motioned that he'd go first. Karl nodded, hanging back a few feet.

As he carefully placed one foot in front of the other, eyes taking in the area ahead, Daniel felt himself slip into his old role, the animal inside begging to be let out. Like a panther stalking its prey, eager with deadly calm, the sniper moved forward.

6:38PM

Eddie Chavez steadied his breathing. It looked like he was going to make first contact. They'd surprised him by moving so quickly. They were either balls to the wall stupid, or supremely confident with their skills.

Chavez didn't care either way. He had enough explosives set up to take out a platoon. That was what he liked to do. Some guys liked long rifle shots, others liked heavy machine guns. Eddie Chavez had always loved the sound of exploding ordnance and the smell of the aftermath. His superiors hadn't liked it much when he'd made the switch from explosive ordnance disposal (EOD) to freelance bomb-maker. He'd killed a shitload of Iraqis before one of his fellow EOD techs ratted him out.

But that fucker had gotten his due. Three days after telling the colonel that SPC Chavez had been sneaking out at night to blow up civilians, he met his maker when a piece of shrapnel nearly severed his head, courtesy of an IED specially rigged by Chavez. He'd gotten out shortly after that, realizing his time was up.

Now he worked for Mason, a commander who truly cherished Chavez's talents. In fact, the explosives for the operations against the Marines were specially designed by Chavez himself. Yeah, he liked working for Mason.

And now, even though he was shivering from the cold, Chavez waited patiently for the enemy to move into his kill zone. He couldn't see them, but he'd set out enough debris that the sound of their passing would give him the cue. It wasn't the way he would've done it, but General Mason had ordered them to have the same handicap as the invaders: no electronics.

Chavez didn't complain because he knew Mason wouldn't listen. Instead he did what he'd always done, improvised. Luckily claymore mines were allowed, one of Chavez's favorite toys. He'd put them to good use before, and was looking forward to doing the same now. So as he hid behind the clump of boulders, gripping the mine trigger, he imagined the carnage that would soon litter the quiet North Carolina countryside.

6:41PM

Daniel found the first claymore as he went to step around a pine sapling. Some people might've called it luck, but if that was the case, Daniel had a way of always being lucky. He knew it was more than that. Something had told him to take a circuitous route toward whatever sound they'd heard. That simple act had probably saved their lives.

He motioned for Karl to go prone and tried to imagine how he might construct the kill zone himself. By the way the claymore was pointing, he and Karl would've walked right into the trap.

After a moment to think, Daniel slung his rifle over his shoulder and pulled the double-edged blade out of its chest sheath. With the stealth of a puma, Daniel prowled into the night.

6:47PM

Chavez shifted his position, careful not to make a sound. He thought for sure that he would've heard them by now. It would be amazing if he could get all six together. That would really make Gen. Mason happy, and would probably piss off that prick Dan. Fuck that guy. He was Mason's favorite, but the guy's coke habit was insane. Chavez was pretty sure the guy went on every Op with a stash of the white stuff. Wasn't getting high on killing enough?

Shit, he thought. *I'll show the general who's best.*

He heard a noise and readied the trigger. The eight claymores would let out a helluva boom. He grinned just thinking about it, straining to hear confirmation of the enemy's presence.

No sooner had he craned his neck around the lowest point of the boulder than something dropped on top of him.

He almost panicked, but remembered the trigger in his hand and went to clack it. It never happened.

Something pressed painfully against his wrist, pinning it against the ground and causing him to release his hold. His wits still with him, Chavez tried to roll away, only to find the eyes of a wild animal staring back, only they were on the face of a man. He didn't have a chance to process any of it because a blade entered his throat and plunged into the base of his brain. Lights out.

6:58PM

It hadn't taken Karl and Daniel long to trace the wire to their corresponding claymores. Karl could feel the sweat running down his back, more from nerves than exhaustion. They'd dodged a big one there. He'd seen what one claymore could do, but eight?

As they hid half of the mines and stashed the rest on their packs, Karl asked, "How did you know?"

Daniel shrugged, his composure the same as if they'd just woken up from a nap. "I just did."

Karl shivered. He couldn't put his finger on it, but there was something about this kid. He'd been through all sorts of nightmare missions in his years in the Army, and he'd served with all levels of operators, but this Briggs was something he'd never seen before: a water walker, not in the derogatory sense, but in the literal 'this one can do anything' sense.

"Ready?" asked Daniel.

"Yeah."

Leaving the concealed body of Mason's bomb maker behind, the two men once again slithered their way south.

———————

7:04PM

It was strange not hearing the soft chatter of your teammates as you moved toward the objective. The absence felt more than a little disconcerting to Gaucho. He wondered if maybe the six should've stayed together. Sure, they were a bigger target, but maneuvering and coordinating would've been much easier, not to mention the combined firepower.

Gaucho took a sip of water from his CamelBack and kept moving. Three steps later, his foot stepped on what looked like a level piece of ground in the shadowed undergrowth, but instead his foot slipped through and he felt himself falling. He tried to wrench himself back, but his momentum was too far forward. Bracing for impact, he bit back the curse that came to his lips.

Suddenly the fall stopped. He could feel his web harness pressing against his chest.

"You okay?" came the low whisper from behind.

"Get me out of here."

MSgt Trent heaved him out of whatever he'd almost fallen into and placed him back on his feet.

"We good?"

"Yeah, thanks to you."

As Trent kept an eye on their surroundings, Gaucho bent down and tried to get a better look at the hole. He winced when he saw the white edges of sharpened tree limbs, better known as punji sticks, a devilish trap made notorious by the Vietcong during the Vietnam War.

The sight of the deadly trap snapped him back, taking in every nook he could see. They'd expected rifle on rifle, not backwoods death dealing.

"Let's get going," said Gaucho.

"You want me out front?"

"I'm good."

With their first surprise behind them, Gaucho and Trent continued on their way.

7:06PM

Abraham Dellow grunted. He was sure he'd gotten the little one. How had the big guy moved so quickly and snatched back his companion? It didn't matter. The punji death trap was only one of many tricks he had up his sleeve. As a native of the North Carolina woods, Dellow felt more at home here than he ever did in the city.

Confident that there were no more than two men in his sector, Dellow climbed down from the deer stand and picked a path a little farther up the draw where he could easily follow the mismatched pair. Dellow licked his chapped lips. Deer hunting had nothing on killing your fellow man.

7:12PM

Gaucho stopped to listen. It was impossible to be totally quiet on a forest bed covered in dried leaves and branches, but at least the wind had picked up and helped mask their movement. He swiveled left and thought he caught a shadow up the steep ridge. There it was again.

MSgt Trent had taken a knee and was looking the same way as Gaucho. The two men looked at each other, Trent raising one finger to indicate a single possible target. Gaucho nodded. Somehow the enemy had gotten behind them.

He weighed the option of just moving forward to hit their timeline, but the thought of falling into another pit kept them from moving too fast. That would give their shadow the advantage. He found a tree that barely masked his form, and took a knee behind it. Maybe a couple minutes of waiting would flush out their tail.

———————

7:15PM

Abraham Dellow had seen the two men stop. As luck would have it, he'd also seen the buck that they were now focused on. The deer had taken his original route and was now picking its way along the ridge line. Nature's perfect diversion.

With the skills that his moonshine brewing grandaddy had taught him, he backtracked and came at them from another angle.

7:19PM

The shadow had disappeared, making Gaucho wonder if it had just been a trick of the night or had actually been the enemy. Like so many other decisions made on the battlefield, his next was pure instinct. He told Trent what he had in mind, and the hulking Marine readily agreed.

7:26PM

Dellow crept from tree to tree, grateful for the wind that had gone from a constant drone to a steady howl. He could see the two forms huddled against a tree, their silhouettes positioned in such a way that he knew they were still oriented up the hill. He was coming from exactly the opposite direction.

They weren't fifty feet away when he raised his rifle and double-tapped them both.

7:27PM

It had been Trent's idea to construct hasty replicas of themselves with their shirts, gear and some brush. They even seemed to move in the gusting breeze.

The muzzle flashes were all they needed. No sooner had the man's fourth shot entered MSgt Trent's doppelganger than both the Marine and Gaucho took him down with matching shots.

They approached the writhing form. Amazingly the man was still alive and trying to crawl away. Normally Willy Trent might've tried to save the man's life, take him in for questioning. But this was no normal mission. Over four hundred of his fellow Marines had been killed. There was a good chance the man they'd shot had been on the ground when it happened. That was all Trent needed to think about at he raised his weapon again, and sent two rounds into the back of the man's head.

7:44PM

Unlike the others, Dan wasn't about to play by the rules. Chavez with his explosives and Dellow with his redneck-Vietcong-Rambo bullshit. While he'd heard the shots earlier (he guessed they were probably at least a click away) and he hoped his side had come out on top, he really didn't care.

He was a survivor. You didn't make it through multiple undercover tours both with Delta and with the CIA without learning that when it came to the question of rules, there were none.

So while the rest of Mason's boys were taking the old school approach, Dan had come prepared. No fucking around with obsolete weaponry. He had the most advanced weapon system money could not yet buy. It was a prototype of a next generation infantry launch system developed by OrionTech. Call it a one man missile silo. Smaller than an

RPG, the weapon was shoulder launched, putting a barrage of tiny high explosive missiles downrange in a matter of seconds. With a max range of just under a mile, the launcher gave a new meaning to the old 'reach out and touch somebody' line. There were twenty rounds per cartridge, but one round alone could take out an entire squad. He'd fallen in love with the lethal contraption the second he'd first touched it on the live-fire range. This one weapon would change the face of infantry tactics for decades to come. It was light, compact and simple to operate.

He raised the twenty pound launcher to his shoulder and looked through the IR scope. As plain as if it were light out, he saw the two forms moving closer, traversing the military crest of a steep hill, coming right to his position. He wanted to wait, let them get a little closer. That way he didn't have to walk too far to see the remains. He'd always wanted to see what the carnage was like after his new favorite weapon cut through the enemy.

7:47PM

Cal and Vince were taking turns at point. They hadn't said more than a few words since stepping off hours ago. There was no need. There were the occasional stops to consult their map, but other than that it was moving and scanning.

They were just dipping below the military crest of a particularly steep hill when Vince signaled a halt. He took a knee and Cal followed suit. They were getting close. He wondered if Daniel and Karl were already to the rendezvous point, and tried to shake the feeling that they were being watched.

7:48PM

Dan watched the two men take a knee. It looked like the one in the lead was checking out his map. *This is too easy*, he thought, caressing the trigger. The shit he did to the Marines in Afghanistan had been fun, but he hadn't been around to see the aftermath. This time he'd get to see it up close and personal, and if everything went according to plan, and Gen. Mason's scheme worked, there would be a lot more killing to be done in the near future.

He patted the launcher lovingly. A few more minutes, and then he could unleash hell.

CHAPTER 38

Gen. Winfield checked his gear as the Osprey banked left. The Sergeant Major of the Marine Corps, SgtMaj Harley Sharp, was doing the same. The grizzled warrior, who had the innate ability to cuss and drink like a sailor, was one of Winfield's favorite people. They'd come into the Corps the same year, serving in their first battalion together. Over the years their paths converged time and again as they stepped higher up the Marine Corps ladder.

He'd chosen SgtMaj Sharp to be the new Sergeant Major of the Marine Corps for one simple reason: he was the best goddamn enlisted Marine he'd ever met. He was Dan Daley reborn. The man cared for his Marines, even though he could be tough as nails, chewing and spitting them out, but the smart ones loved him back.

When Sharp had heard about what the Commandant was planning, he volunteered at once. Winfield was glad he had. There wasn't much chance of them getting into a fire-fight, but he felt it was important to have the senior officer and senior enlisted man of the Corps on deck when things were resolved.

The other services had come to his call. With the help of the Chairman of the Joint Chiefs, his good friend Gen. McMillan, they'd conversed via conference call. In true joint service fashion, and after an impassioned speech from McMillan, the other heads of their respective services opened their doors to Winfield. He was overwhelmed by their generosity, and promised himself that he would do more in the future to help them in return.

So as they flew into enemy territory, emboldened by the fact that they now had Gen. Ellwood's files and no longer needed the confession from Mason, Winfield felt like a young Marine lieutenant again. He and his men were against the enemy, hoping to make it in time to save more Marine lives.

7:54PM

It had been the Air Force Chief of Staff who'd recommended the most crucial addition to the plan. While they didn't know what kind of anti-air defense Mason had up his sleeve, the Joint Chiefs were loath to commence an all-out aerial attack on U.S. soil.

"I suggest we use an EMP," the Air Force general had said.

"In North Carolina? That's insane!" the Chief of Naval Operation replied. "That could wipe out the electric grid for thousands."

The Air Force general, gave his colleague a sly grin. "We have recently developed a localized EMP smart bomb that can be tailored to an area of our choosing. That means that as long as we know what we want to black out, we can do it rather effectively."

There'd been some further questions about why the others didn't know about the new technology and how exactly it would work, but in the end, and with the blessing of the president, they all agreed that it was worth the risk.

The delivery vehicle was a clone of a commercial airliner, complete with US Airways lettering and a valid tail number. It was already rigged for military use and even had a fully functioning bomb bay. Using the commercial plane would mask their intent in the eyes of Gen. Mason and his anti-aircraft pods.

"Target acquired," the bombardier announced over the PA system. A moment later, the orange painted smart bomb left the plane and dropped toward terra firma.

7:56PM

Cal flinched when the explosion went off in the sky, illuminating the area for a few seconds.

"What the hell was that?" he asked.

"No idea," answered Vince, who was stuffing the map back in his pocket. "One of Mason's surprises?"

Cal shrugged. "Let's get back on the road."

They moved out, neither man glancing at their watches. If they had, they would have noticed that they were no longer working.

The screen in the eyepiece went dark. Dan shook the launcher and tried clicking the reset button. Nothing.

He tried replacing the battery, but that didn't work either.

It was just his luck that the damn thing went down just as he was settling in for the shot. He'd have to give the engineers a piece of his mind when it was all over. They promised him that the weapon was "grunt proof," but apparently that wasn't the case.

Dan pulled out a pair of night vision goggles, glad that he'd brought them along. They didn't have near the range of the launcher's scope, but it was better than nothing.

He took off the lens cap and put the goggles to his eyes, flicking the ON switch. Nothing but black.

What the…?

Dread suddenly crept up his back. He grabbed the cell phone from his cargo pocket and tried to make a call. It was dead.

The confidence he'd felt minutes earlier swept away. He picked up his weapon and decided the most prudent thing to do was head back the way he'd come. Maybe Mason knew what was going on.

As he picked his way through the trees, he heard a sound that unnerved him even more, making him break into a trot. There was a helicopter coming, and by the sound of it, it was coming in fast.

The Army UH-60 Blackhawk thundered over the treetops.

"We've got a runner," announced the co-pilot.

The Marine Raider, who'd done his first stint in the Marine Corps as a scout sniper, peered through his scope. "I've got him," he said to his platoon commander, who was watching the scene through his own optics.

"Take him."

The sergeant exhaled slowly, and pulled the trigger.

Dan had just hopped over a log when the sniper's bullet hit him in the back. He was conscious long enough to feel his face slam into the cold earth and then see the Blackhawk fly overhead. He was already fading when the machine gun rounds from the door gunner pulverized his body.

The Blackhawk circled over Cal and Vince. Cal motioned south to a spot he knew they could land. The nose of the helo tilted forward, and off it went.

"Well, at least we won't have to walk much farther," said Cal.

"Yeah. Let's go see what's cookin'."

CHAPTER 39

By the time the Blackhawk landed near the row of Quonset huts, the mop-up was complete. On the way, the captain in charge of the Marine Raider contingent had given Cal a run-down of the Commandant's plan and told him that Mason's remaining men in the field had been eliminated.

From the EMP supplied by the Air Force, to the Delta commandos, Marine Raiders, and Navy SEALs, this had been a true joint effort. All the bad guys except for Mason had been taken care of, and the rest of Cal's men were on their way in.

Cal stepped off the helo and headed over to where Gen. Winfield was conversing with a couple of black clad opera-tors, most likely Delta, and another man in cammies who had his back turned to Cal. One of the operators motioned towards Cal and Winfield turned.

"I'm glad to see you made it in one piece," said Winfield, shaking Cal's hand.

"I guess I have you to thank for that, sir. You want to tell me what changed between us getting here and you guys flying in to save the day?"

Winfield told him about Diane's discovery and how the contents of Ellwood's files were now being used to round up the perpetrators, including the men Mason had assigned to take care of certain Marine units around the world.

"So that's it? We have everything?"

"We have Mason, his men, and the military officers who contributed to Steiner's report. It turns out that Doug Ellwood was quite the amateur sleuth."

"Did he leave any indication about why he took his own life?" Cal asked. To him it was still the strangest part of the saga.

Winfield nodded sadly. "Long story short, General Ellwood found out about the scheme when a drunk Gower tried to enlist his old friend's help. He later tried to deny it, saying it was a joke, but Doug started digging and used every contact he had to get the information. Gower and Mason caught wind of what he was doing and threatened to not only tie him to the plot, but kill his family. They told him that the only way he could save his Marines and his family was to take his own life. I don't think they found out about the file until after he was dead."

"He was a good man, sir, a Marine's Marine," said the gray-haired man standing across from Winfield in matching forest green utilities.

"That he was, Sergeant Major. I'm sorry I ever thought ill of him," said Winfield. "Cal, I don't think you've met Sergeant Major Sharp. I just appointed him our new Sergeant Major of the Marine Corps."

"Cal Stokes, Sergeant Major. Congratulations on the new job."

"Thank you. I guess I just couldn't say no to one more ride in the bull's ring with my old platoon commander," said Sharp. He looked like he could've been close to eighty, with the weathered face of the Marlboro Man.

"What happened to Mason?" asked Cal.

"The general is waiting for you," answered Winfield.

"Me? Why?"

"He says he's got your reward, that you won, even though you didn't fight fair."

"Is he armed?"

Winfield nodded. "I don't think he'll pull a Custer, but he wants his last hoorah. He said he wants to keep his weapon at his side."

"I'll go talk to him."

"We'll come with you," said Winfield, motioning for SgtMaj Sharp to follow.

Cal walked up to the Quonset hut that was now surrounded by operators. They let the three Marines pass.

Someone had set out a path of orange chem lights leading from the door of the warehouse to the spacious office. There was a kerosene lamp on the desk. It cast a yellow glow over the room, and illuminated only half of Gen. Mason's face. He was sitting in his desk chair, puffing on a pungent cigar, his rifle leaning against the wall next to him.

"There he is, the conquering hero," said Mason, throwing a mock salute Cal's way.

"What do you want?" asked Cal.

"I figured we should see each other one last time, man to man."

"Say what you want to say."

"Okay. I'll bet you're wondering why I did it. Why did I throw away a good career and ruin a lot of people's lives, right?"

Cal didn't respond.

Mason continued. "I'll tell you why, and Winfield, you and your lapdog may want to listen. The second we take off our uniforms, we're one of them. Weak civilians who suck off the teat that our warriors provide. We can't turn back time and do it again. We're old and used up. There's nothing I wouldn't give to go back and do it again, to lead a platoon or even pick up a rifle as a private. But the chain of command is broken, gents. The ranks are filled with war fighters with the hearts of lions. What are we but a bunch of weathered relics? Well I didn't want to go out that way. I still have fight left. So I had to kill a few people to get there. So what? People die every single day."

Cal didn't buy it. "And why the Marine Corps, why General Ellwood?"

"They tried to recruit me to be a Marine out of Annapolis. Did you know that? Well, I realized they already had their shining star. Doug Ellwood could do no wrong. He got the prettiest girl and somehow won the most awards. So I decided to take another path, to make my own way. But that didn't help. Doug kept one step ahead of me. It's no secret that he probably would've been Commandant one day. So when the opportunity came, when Gower told me what he was thinking, I pushed it as hard as I could. Gower thought he was the one with the MacArthur brain, but I was the one who came up with the plan. I was the one who took it to a whole other level."

"And Steiner? How does he play into this?"

Mason laughed. "He's just a pansy politician. He didn't know we were behind it. We took recipes that have been simmering for years and spoon fed it to him. You wouldn't believe how many people in the Army, Air Force and Navy would love to see you Marines gone."

Cal wondered if there'd ever be a time when the egos of man wouldn't disrupt the lives of others. He knew it was impossible, and reminded himself that he was one of the few people on the planet who could do something about maniacs like Mason.

"Is that all?" asked Cal.

Mason nodded, taking a long drag from his stubby cigar.

Gen. Winfield stared at the man who'd been behind the murder of so many of his Marines. It was unconscionable, treasonous, pure evil. Part of him wanted to pull out his pistol and shoot the man full of lead.

Mason looked at him with an amused grin, and then shifted back to Cal.

"Semper Fucking Fi," Mason drawled, then shifted his weight forward just perceptibly.

Winfield's eyes narrowed as his gaze followed Mason's movement. He wasn't going for his weapon, but he did tap his boot on the floor. A split second later a loud CLICK sounded. Gen. Winfield didn't hesitate. He knew what was coming. He pushed past Cal just as the bouncing betty anti-personnel mine popped up from an invisible hole in the ground.

Everything slowed. Mason just sat there, unblinking, watching the show, knowing he would die. Winfield felt a presence behind him and realized at the last possible moment that it was Harley Sharp, his old friend, his trusted advisor, with him 'til the end. Winfield somehow caught the anti-personnel mine and held it to his chest. SgtMaj Sharp started to wrap his arms around Winfield as the bomb went off. Roaring chaos shattered the room and left only one man breathing.

EPILOGUE

The near freezing temperatures did little to shake the resolve of the overflowing crowd. They'd come as one to mourn their lost brothers. Old Marines in wheelchairs sat next to Marine amputees who'd served in Iraq and Afghanistan. Pot bellied motorheads, Marine emblems proudly displayed on their leather jackets and tattoos stood arm and arm with active duty Marines in blues and greens. They stood stoically, tragically accustomed to the loss of comrades.

The sun peeked out from behind the cloud just as President Zimmer took the podium. He was joined by the Joint Chiefs who stood a respectful step behind him. The political supporters included the vice president, the president's chief of staff, Travis Haden and Congressman Tony McKnight. The politicians each wore a small Marine pin on their lapels.

Cal watched from the middle of the crowd, the bandage on his head covered by a grey beanie. Diane stood next to him, her hand wrapped around his. Daniel, MSgt Trent and

235

Gaucho were with them, as were Neil, Jonas and Dr. Higgins. They'd all come to pay their collective respects, to remember the lives tragically cut short, and the selfless sacrifices of others.

"Today we gather to remember the fallen," the president began, looking out over the crowd. "Heroes like General Scotty Winfield, Sergeant Major Harley Sharp and General Doug Ellwood. These Marines epitomized what it means to be a leader, what it means to be an American. I don't think any one of them would have said they were perfect, but goddammit, they were Marines."

The cheer went up from the once hushed crowd. This was a side of Zimmer that America had rarely seen. He waited for the Oorahs, whistles and shouts to subside.

"These men gave their lives for others. Not only did they dedicate their careers in service of this country, but they believed in the quality of man and that freedom is something that we all deserve.

"Over the past few weeks, I had the great honor to get to know General Winfield. He was a man with an unflinching loyalty for his Marines and his country. He believed that the Marine Corps saved his life and had the ability to do the same for young men and women now and in the future. The Marine Corps was his home, where he chose to hang his sword. He said he was proudest of the legacy of the Marine Corps, the leaders it had produced and the enemies it held at bay. But he was also concerned about its future. He told me that selfishness and a cancerous sense of entitlement not only threatened the foundation of the Marine Corps, but of its sister services and the entire country.

"These flag officers standing behind me are a testament to the vision General Winfield had. He believed in a United States military that lived up to the traditions of old. Honor. Sacrifice. Loyalty. Today we pledge to live up to his ideal, to work together, to mend our wounds and forge our bonds. The Secretary of Defense, with the help of the Joint Chiefs will work to build a new foundation of joint cooperation. While a soldier may be a soldier, and a Marine is always a Marine, we are all Americans, united in a common cause in the defense of this great nation.

"As we mourn the loss of your brothers, we must also take a step forward, and look to the future. I am happy to tell you, that this afternoon, at the home of the Marine Corps at Eighth & I streets, your new commandant will take his oath."

There were murmurs throughout the crowd. No one had heard about the announcement. They were shocked that some higher up had chosen to replace Gen. Winfield so soon.

President Zimmer nodded to the crowd, acknowledging that he understood their confusion.

"I've taken this unprecedented step with the full support of your top officer and senior enlisted leaders. I'm happy to say that I didn't have to look far for General Winfield's successor. Your new Commandant was not only a very good friend of General Winfield, and was held in high esteem by his old comrade, but comes with plenty of experience. I won't keep you waiting, I promise. Marines, ladies and gentlemen, I am honored to tell you that the next Commandant of the Marine Corps, a man I greatly admire, and am proud to call a valued advisor and friend, is General McMillan."

There was a pause as the crowd tried to process who General McMillan was. The only one they knew was currently the Chairman of the Joint Chiefs, the senior officer in the entire United States Armed Forces. Was there another McMillan? Their answer came a moment later, when the four-star general replaced the president at the podium. The crowd erupted in cheers. This was completely unprecedented. Up until recently, there'd never been a Marine who'd served in America's highest military post. Now he was stepping back, taking his stars to the Corps?

Gen. McMillan put up his hand, silencing the crowd.

"Thank you for the warm welcome. I know Scotty Winfield is looking down on us now, smiling at you and waggling his finger at me. I know exactly what he'd say. too. Don't screw it up, Mac!"

The crowd laughed and their soon-to-be Commandant chuckled with them. He looked up at the sky.

"We'll miss you, old friend. Semper Fidelis."

Gen. McMillan kept it short, thanking the president and the heads of the Army, Navy and Air Force. Once his speech concluded, he stepped off the stage and went to mingle with the crowd. Congressman McKnight watched him go.

"Thanks again for coming, Tony," said the president, patting McKnight on the back.

"There's no place I'd rather be, Mr. President."

"Anyway, it means a lot to me that you came. Thanks again for the support. I won't forget it." The president nodded to the head of his security detail and he was swept away in an orderly fashion.

McKnight looked out over the crowd and then his eyes followed the wailing sirens of the D.C. cops escorting the president back to the White House. Despite his neutral demeanor, McKnight could only repeat one question over and over again in his head, "How did it go wrong?"

He'd had every piece in place. There was overwhelming pressure coming at the president and Marine Corps from all sides. How the hell had Zimmer slipped through the gauntlet once again?

His pawns had failed. Gower and Mason were dead. Tom Steiner was still in FBI custody. And Glen Whitworth was hiding behind his lawyers as agencies pounced on OrionTech. It seemed that whatever Gen. Ellwood uncovered in his covert investigation included information about the Whitworth family's illegal business dealings. Words like bribery, extortion and even murder were being tossed around the upper echelons of those in the know. It would take Whitworth a long time to dig out of his own mess, if he even could.

McKnight took a deep breath of chilly December air and told himself that it didn't matter. He'd suffered setbacks before, but he had plenty of time to prep for the presidential election, and there were many more pawns for him to use. In fact, he already had a plan in place that would tip the scales in his direction. All he needed was a little time.

I hope you've enjoyed this story.
If you did, please take a moment to write an honest review. Your reviews fuel this book's success and are much appreciated.

TO GET A FREE COPY OF ANY *CORPS JUSTICE* NOVEL AND HEAR ABOUT NEW RELEASES: >> http://CorpsJustice.com <<

TO SEE ALL BOOKS IN THE CORPS JUSTICE SERIES:
http://CorpsJustice.com

DID YOU FIND AN ERROR? REPORT
IT TO THE GRAMMAR POLICE!
http://www.corpsjustice.com/grammar-police.html

MORE THANKS TO MY BETA READERS:
Cheryl, Don D., Susan, Don H., Pam, Glenda, Shawn, Alex, Nancy, Kathy, Marsha, D.M., Len, CaryLory, Doug and David, you guys are awesome. Thanks for keeping me on my toes.

Made in the USA
Monee, IL
19 June 2020